The Vigilante

W.R. Hill

1

For Mom and Dad

Miss you both very much.

Chapter 1

It was a moonless January night; the kind of night where the cold chills you to the bone. The only light was a dim street lamp three blocks away from where Addison sat in her four year old black Lexus watching the drug dealer. She'd wanted to buy a new car but her ever practical husband, Morgan, had won out. "Why buy new? The minute you drive it off the lot the value goes down at least ten percent or more," he said. So they bought the used Lexus instead of the new GMC Yukon she'd had her eye on. She didn't put up much of an argument. She loved him too much to argue over something like a car.

Addison Cooper is one of those rare, stunningly beautiful women. Heads turn when she walks into a room. It doesn't matter if it's the lobby of a theater and she's wearing that little size six form fitting black sequined dress, or if she is in a grocery store aisle wearing sweats, running shoes, and no makeup. She stands a fraction over five-six, and weighs a trim one-twenty. Her milky white skin and natural red hair are accentuated by pale green eyes; eyes that can look right through you. Eyes that can see fear and instantly spot a lie without offering so much as a blink. Eyes that can see what you're thinking. These are the eyes of a killer with a third degree black belt in Aikido and an ability to accurately shoot the most sophisticated of weapons from hand guns to sniper rifles and everything in between. She's as comfortable with a Black Hawk military tactical knife as most women are with a hair brush. She has an eidetic memory and an IQ close to the one-sixty mark. She left the CIA's secret Looking Glass unit eight years earlier after she was nearly killed in an operation that ended badly and left her in critical condition with a long road to recovery. She'd hoped to leave that life behind forever but fate had intervened. Now she was back and on a mission more important than any she'd been involved with in the past.

The drug dealer was in his element. This was his turf, his territory, his office. He worked a corner on the southern edge of Chicago's upscale, Portage Park neighborhood. Addison watched transaction after transaction through her AN/PVS-5 Night Vision optics. The nine thousand dollar night eyes were one of the many toys she kept when she left the CIA. She watched as car after car from the affluent surroundings pulled to the curb. The drug dealing entrepreneur would walk to the driver's side door with his hands in his pockets. He'd hunch up his shoulders to ward off the cold and casually look up and down the deserted icy street. His right hand would come out of his pocket and go palm up through the driver's window. The hand would come back full of cash. At the same time his left hand would come out of his pocket holding a small clear plastic bag filled with white powder which was handed to the driver. Devon T. Washington was a well oiled, finely tuned, drug dealing machine. A machine that wore expensive new Nike shoes and a black hooded Nike sweatshirt with the hood pulled up. A pair of expensive Calvin Kline jeans completed the ensemble. Devon was a drug dealer with expensive tastes and an eye for fashion. Each time his back turned towards Addison she could see the small bulge at the waistband in the middle of his back. That was what she was after.

She was looking for a weapon that came from the streets, the streets where a ten year old could get a gun if he had the right connections. She had come upon the drug dealer purely by chance. She was cruising around the affluent neighborhood without any particular plan when the opportunity presented itself. She saw the slick looking guy standing on the corner leaning against a car that had just driven up. You didn't have to be Sherlock Holmes to see what was going on. She drove around the block once and parked three blocks away to watch the guy. Her suspicions were confirmed in just a few minutes.

Addison unbuttoned the top two buttons of her blouse, started the car and drove to the corner to meet the young entrepreneur. She lowered her window as the car came to a stop. "Hey pretty momma, whassup? Ain't seen you around here before," the young thug said as he stepped off the curb and up to the car window.

"You've got something I want," Addison replied.

"Don't know what you talkin bout lady," he said as he peered down at her cleavage. "Tell you what though, I be glad to give you some of what I got for some of what you got," he said as his empty hand reached through the window and came to rest on her right breast, exactly what she'd hoped for. She raised her left hand and grabbed his wrist. "What is it with guys and women's breasts?" she said as she moved her left hand up into his forearm and grabbed his turned down palm with her right hand causing him to let go of her. Next, with her left hand she pushed his elbow straight up. Ikkyo, the first step you learn in Akaido. The pain in the drug dealer's wrist from the pressure on his ulnar nerve was excruciating. He started dropping to his knees, looking for a way to escape the agony. As he was going down, she let go and quickly opened the door slamming it into his body. He fell sideways, like a ten pin hit dead on for a strike.

"Geez bitch, what you do that for? I was only going for a little feel."

She used the heel of her left foot to push him the rest of the way down onto his stomach. She put her right foot on the back of his neck, pinning his face to the pavement. She casually reached down and took the gun from beneath his waistband. "This is what I came for," she said, as she lifted her foot off his neck and stepped back. He pulled his knees up and began to stand when she used the weapon to slap him in the side of the head. He went down for the count. She hurried back to the warmth of the Lexus, took a minute to scan the area for anyone that may have seen what happened and drove off.

Chapter 2

Addison had left New Hampshire two days earlier on January first at three in the morning. She'd headed south then west, with no real destination in mind, driving into a New Year, and new life. A new life in which she had nothing left to lose. The two most important people in her life were gone forever. Her husband, Morgan, had been taken from her six months earlier.

Morgan fought it as best he could, but the monster ravishing his body had too much of a head start in the race. He'd noticed a few extra body aches and pains which he attributed to getting a little older and his fairly constant physical labor. He was working in the yard when the pain hit that brought the disease clearly into focus. He'd just reached down to pick up a pair of pruning shears when he suddenly felt as though his stomach had been ripped open. His knees buckled as he fell to the ground from the intense pain. Addison was looking through the kitchen window and saw him fall. The glass dish she was holding crashed to the floor as she dropped it and rushed to his side. He tried but was unable to speak, just breathing took every ounce of strength he had. Addison took the phone out of his shirt pocket and dialed 911 as he lay on the ground writhing in pain. She held his head in her lap desperately trying to comfort him as they waited for the ambulance.

The doctors said it was a fast growing, aggressive cancer of the worst kind. The prognosis had not been good, six months to a year they said. They were wrong. Her beloved Morgan died two months to the day after his diagnosis, with Addison sitting at his bedside holding his hand.

A few years earlier, Addison had purchased an old house in a quiet neighborhood in Wilson, New Hampshire. The house had been an absolute wreck but despite that there was lots of character. The home had clearly been neglected for many years. It was a two story with a basement and a wraparound porch and a huge shade tree in the front yard. You could see sky through the ceiling and dirt through the floor in some parts of the old place. She'd been looking for a project, something to do, something as far removed from her old occupation as a she could get. The dilapidated old house fit the bill and she was able to pick it up for a song. The former owner had been an old spinster with few heirs and no will. After her death it took a city clerk several months to track down a shirt tail relative in Redding, California that had no interest in the property. He let it sit for six years before finally listing it with a local realtor over the phone.

Addison hired a handsome carpenter to provide labor for the heavy work, and to do the finish carpentry. Morgan Wright had been a charmer from the very beginning. He had calloused hands, weathered skin from working outdoors and a body that was hard as nails. His hair was brown and a little shaggy. He was an excellent craftsman with a contagious smile beneath piercing blue eyes that

9

reminded Addison of Paul Newman. Tiny crow's feet were beginning to creep out of the corners of his eyes. He had an optimism that would make you think you could do anything in the world. He never saw the down side of things, only the greatest of possibilities that lay just around the corner. It was an optimism and enthusiasm that came in handy as they labored on the old house.

They married after a whirlwind courtship and the two of them worked side by side for the next eight months to complete the remodel. Being a modern, liberated woman, Addison chose to keep her own last name. A year later Joey was born. Addison never told Morgan the truth about her previous life. He thought she'd taught English in several foreign countries before settling in New Hampshire. She explained the numerous scars on her body as the result of an automobile accident caused by huge quantities of alcohol and poor judgment during her early college years. Theirs was the fairy tale existence that she'd dreamt about as a precocious twelve year old girl, long before the CIA had turned her into a killer.

Their son Joey inherited his dad's personality and his mother's looks. He was always positive and believed he could do anything. He was slender with his mother's pale skin and red hair set off by a sea of freckles on an ever smiling, mischievous face. His hair was always a mess from his constant running around chasing balls, and wrestling with his playful dad. He was five and had just started kindergarten when his father died. He had a hard time grasping what had happened. He couldn't understand why daddy left and never came back. Addison fought back tears on a nightly basis when Joey asked when daddy was coming home. Several months went by and Joey began to understand. Addison channeled away some of her grief by focusing more on Joey. She hugged him harder and looked at him longer as the days slowly passed by. Then it happened, the unthinkable, a school shooting. Addison had dropped Joey off at school that day like she always did. She made him give her a hug and as usual she held him a little longer. She handed him his sack lunch and watched him run up the steps into the school. He reached the top of the steps, turned and gave her a big smile and a wave before disappearing through the school doors. That was the last time Addison saw her son alive.

It was a small school with high standards that routinely produced some of the best and brightest kids in the district. The entire staff was dedicated to providing an excellent education to the five hundred children in the kindergarten through fourth grade facility. The school was in a picturesque New England setting surrounded by rolling hills thick with maple, birch, hickory and other deciduous trees. Most of the leaves were gone, but the beauty of the countryside remained. The American flag waved gently in the morning breeze high atop the flagpole as the yellow buses lined up in the drive dropping kids off. They were all greeted with open arms and warm hugs from the school's teachers.

Two hours later Joey, along with several other kids and adults, lay dead, their young lives cut short by a crazed lunatic carrying a small arsenal.

The authorities peeled back layers as best they could looking for clues that made a young man snap and suddenly go on a homicidal rampage. Evan James Weatherford was 19 at the time of the shooting. He was tall and slender with large round inquisitive eyes and a mop of dark brown hair. Like many others of his generation, he'd grown up in a family broken apart by divorce. Mom had been a social worker and dad a corporate executive. They divorced when Evan was 13 and Mrs. Weatherford got custody of their only child. Evan was pretty edgy growing up and didn't like to be touched. As he grew older he developed a fascination with guns and spent countless hours with his mother at the local shooting range learning to shoot a variety of weapons. As the years passed he had more and more difficulties at school. He left high school mid-way through his junior year. After that he spent most of his time alone in his dark bedroom playing violent video games. The signs of Evan's instability were present, but there were no laws in place regarding guns in a household. A thorough background check of family members would have shown potential issues that could arise with so many weapons in the home.

Evan arrived at his old school a little after nine-thirty that morning and found the main entry locked. The lock was no match for the 20 gauge Mossberg Model 500 shotgun he used to shoot his way into the building. He went into the first classroom he came to and killed Joey, one other student and a teacher, Frances Armstead. Miss Armstead had been a substitute teacher that day after Joey's regular teacher had called in sick. The young shooter moved to the next classroom where he used a 10 mm Glock 20 SF to kill three more students and a second teacher before heading to the school library where two more students and the librarian lost their lives. He ended the spree by killing the school's janitor and principal as they rushed into the library to investigate. His last act that day was to use the Glock to kill himself.

A week later, little Joey was buried in a simple grave next to his father. After an austere service, Addison went home and closed all the shades in the house. Her devastated mood was matched only by the darkness that surrounded her. A few people came by to drop off food and offer condolences. None stayed very long and none were invited inside. All were people that meant well but they were mostly folks Addison didn't know. She and Morgan hadn't made many friends in the small town. They were content being with each other and raising Joey. She would answer the door in a daze, just staring outside, not really knowing, or caring who the person was, barely able to thank them for their offering. It was all she could do to get off the couch and go to the door.

She'd sobbed, cried, and screamed at the unfairness of it all for nearly a week. She finally reached the point of exhaustion and slept. She woke up angry. Her perfect world had been destroyed, gone forever. The world had gone mad. Guns were everywhere and far too easy to get. The lack of gun controls was appalling and no one was doing anything about it. Something had to be done. People had to be made to understand what was going on. Congress continually turned a blind eye to the problem while filling their pockets with the unlimited funds from the likes of the National Rifle Association that filtered in through avenues. Gun advocates in nearly every state were constantly introducing legislation, often with the backing of the NRA that made owning a gun easier than ever. Politicians seeking sensible gun regulations were quickly voted out of office.

Chapter 3

One of the daily joys for Evelyn Baker is picking up the mail dropped through the slot in front door of the opulent home she and her husband, Supreme Court Justice Harold Baker, own in the exclusive Georgetown suburb of Washington, D.C. The home is a totally refurbished Victorian built in 1890. It's an elegant two story affair with four bedrooms, three baths and three fireplaces, the perfect place for a Supreme Court Justice and his wife to entertain D.C.'s elite. They paid just over three million in cash for the elegant residence shortly after he was appointed to the Supreme Court. Evelyn is an attractive 63 year old who maintains her hour glass figure and has a natural beauty usually highlighted with minimal amounts of makeup. In her younger days she had the face and figure of a high fashion model. Only she and her hair dresser knew the true color of her currently blonde hair. She goes to the gym three days a week, then has coffee with friends afterwards to talk about and add to the latest gossip traveling the beltline around D.C. at lightning speed.

She stood quietly in the foyer sorting through the mail that had just arrived. There were the usual utility bills that came at this time of the month, a couple of coupons advertising great deals on yard maintenance, a letter from an old Yale Law School friend, and a death threat addressed to her husband.

"Anything interesting?" Harold called out from the kitchen where he was making himself a cappuccino on his recently acquired Jura Impressa Z7 espresso maker. He'd paid just over two grand for high tech chrome plated, tricked out top of the line machine a few weeks earlier and loved making specialty coffees for himself and anyone else he could drag into the kitchen.

"Oh the usual, a few bills, some advertisements, a letter from Karen Dickson and what looks like something from someone who wants to kill you," she responded.

"Just put it in the stack with the others. I'll take it to the office on Monday and give it to the Court Police Department. They can decide if they want to pass it on to the Marshall's office."

The first time Justice Baker received a death threat was just after his second year as a Supreme Court Justice. Someone had a beef with the way he'd sided on an environmental issue. Now in his fourteenth year as a Justice he'd received more death threats than he could count, all on a variety of decisions he and his colleagues had handed down over the years. It wasn't uncommon for a Justice to receive a death threat now and then, but all his judicial colleagues agreed he held the record for the most hate mail.

"This one is different from the usual ones," she said. "This one threatens to kill me and one of your brothers as well."

"What?" he said as he walked into the foyer sipping his cappuccino. "Let me see it."

She handed him the letter as he placed his reading glasses hanging around his neck onto the bridge of his long prominent slender nose. He'd always been a little self conscious of his nose and had grown a mustache as soon as he was old enough to shave to help offset the distracting facial feature. His feeling was the cookie duster somehow seemed to shorten the length of his snout. He had bushy eyebrows, a round Charlie Brown face and thinning grey hair. Unlike his lovely wife, Harold was a little on the plump side. Aside from high caloric coffee drinks he had a weakness for sweets and pastries of all kinds. There was a never ending dish of Peanut M&M's on the corner of his desk at home and at his office. He read the letter: *Honorable Scumbag Harry Baker, you have voted the wrong way for the last time. It is clear that big oil and money mean more to you and your dumb ass colleagues than the environment. You have been warned before. Now we must take action. We are going to kill one of your brothers and his family, and then we are coming for you. We're going to kill your wife and cut her into pieces while you watch, then we will cut out your tongue and kill you too.* There was no signature.

"Hmm," he said. This one is over the line. I don't mind the occasional death threat, but when these bozos start threatening my family, something has to be done. I'll give this one to the Director of the U.S. Marshal's office personally." He dropped the letter onto the stack with the others that had arrived that week and took another sip of his coffee concoction. "Our decision against Franklin and his billionaire buddies seems to have caused quite a frenzy in the tree hugging, community," he said as he picked up the letter to give it a second look. "I'll bet this one came from Oregon," he said as he checked the postmark. "That's where most of those side show do-gooder, trust fund, hippie circus freaks hang out." He waved the letter in the air to emphasize his point. "No good bastards," he mumbled as he tossed the letter on the stack and stomped back into the kitchen. "I'm going to make myself another cappuccino, do you want one?"

Evelyn and Harold met when they were both in their first year of law school at Yale. Harold's father and his two brothers, all die-hard republican conservatives, were Yale graduates. Baker's two brothers, one older and one younger, opted for business school. Neither had any desire to join their dad's prestigious law firm in Dallas, Texas where they all grew up. Wynn Baker was the senior partner of Baker, Barker, and Beeker. A somewhat comical name that had evolved as Wynn had expanded over the years. Even with the odd name it was a firm feared by many competing firms in the Dallas area. Any young Texas law school graduate would have given their first born child for a slot as an 80 hour a week associate at B,B and B. Harold's older brother Dan was a hedge fund manager on Wall Street and had more money than he could spend in two lifetimes. The youngest Baker brother, Robert, owned a very successful landscaping business that catered to several hundred wealthy clients throughout the Dallas Metroplex. While Harold and Dan sought money fame and power, Robert sought sunshine, physical labor and the great outdoors.

After law school Harold joined his father's law firm as a senior associate, giving him a closer step to partner. None of the other first year associates held it against him. They all knew it was inevitable and simply kept their heads down and stayed busy trying to prove themselves. The more astute of the bunch, of course, would suck up to Harold at every opportunity. None wanted to be too far behind when the top dog's kid hit the big time. Harold quickly excelled at everything he did knowing he had to perform at a higher standard being a member of the family. He became a partner in three years and was introduced to all the right people in Dallas. The firm and Harold in particular, were great contributors to all local and regional conservative candidates. They made maxim contributions made to George W. Bush in his bid for the presidency in 2000. Shortly after Bush took office in 2001 a vacancy came up in the U.S. District Court in Northern Texas. Bush repaid the financial favors by nominating Harold for the position and he was quickly confirmed after a quick set of Senate Judiciary Committee hearings. A few short years later he took a step up to the Fifth Circuit Court of Appeals in New Orleans and a short while later George W. nominated him once again, only this time to the highest court in the land.

Baker's father died while Harold was an appellate judge in the Fifth Circuit. The three brothers inherited their dad's share of the law firm which they all promptly sold to the remaining law partners. Harold and Evelyn had used a portion of their share to pay cash for the Georgetown house. In addition to leaving his share of the firm to the sons, Wynn had seen fit to take out a six million dollar life insurance policy shortly after joining his dad's law firm naming each of his three sons as beneficiaries.

Early the next morning Justice Baker had his chauffeur drive him directly to the headquarters of the U.S. Marshal's office just across the Potomac in Northern Virginia. While Justices don't normally have chauffeurs, Baker's wealth allowed for such a luxury. Baker called Bill Hardy, the director of the Marshal's office from the limousine on the way. Hardy, an old friend of Bakers', was glad to clear a half hour off his calendar to talk to the Justice.

The office of the U.S. Marshals, a federal agency housed within the Department of Justice, is the oldest American federal law enforcement group. The agency is the law enforcement arm of the U.S. District court system. Their purview covers protection of officers of the courts, fugitive operations, federal arrest warrants and the famous witness protection program. The agency actually came into existence when President George Washington signed the Judiciary Act into law in September of 1798. Many of the first Marshals came from the ranks of military men who fought in the American Revolution. Wyatt Earp was perhaps one of the best known U.S. Marshals.

As soon as he arrived, Baker was ushered straight into the Director's office. Bill Hardy had been a Marshal for over 20 years and worked his way up through the ranks. He had been a serious athlete at his old high school in Frisco, Texas where he was a champion wrestler in the heavy weight class. The same athleticism served him well when he attended Baylor University on a full wrestling scholarship. Many years out of college, he was still in great physical shape and spent two hours each day in the gym working out with weights. Hardy was all muscle packaged in a nearly six foot frame. He had a square jaw line, a broad nose and hair shaved close to the scalp. He wore a dark gray pinstripe suit, with a white shirt and yellow silk tie. Baker and Hardy met while Baker was a judge in one of the Texas Circuit courts where Hardy served as a U.S. Marshal.

Hardy rose from behind his desk and met Baker midway. The two shook hands and sat opposite each other in comfortable leather chairs with a coffee table set between them. A secretary came in with a tray holding a pot of coffee along with cream and sugar containers, two cups and an assortment of cookies.

"So what's all this stuff about death threats? I thought you were used to them by now after all these years on the bench," Hardy said as he picked up the coffee and poured them each a cup. Baker took his and added several ounces of cream and two spoons of sugar and picked up two of the cookies.

"Well, I am, but this latest one goes beyond any of the usual ones I have gotten before," Baker replied as he took the letter out of the inside pocket of his jacket. He had placed the letter and the envelope it came in inside of a plastic zip-lock bag to avoid any further contamination of possible fingerprints.

Hardy retrieved a pair of latex gloves from his desk, put them on and removed the letter from the bag. He read the letter through twice as Baker sat munching on the cookies before placing it back into the zip lock. "You're right about it being different than most of what we see. The unfortunate part about it is that we don't have the manpower to assign someone to track down the people behind the threat. What I can do, however, is help you find someone qualified to look into just what the hell is going on."

"Anything you can do would be greatly appreciated."

"Let me make some calls and I'll get back to you in a day or so."

The two of them spent a few more minutes reminiscing about the old days in Texas while they finished their coffee.

As soon as Baker left, Hardy picked up his phone and called Alan Blackwell, another old friend. Blackwell was the director of the CIA's National Clandestine Service. In Washington, D.C. everyone in the higher levels of government spent a lot of time cultivating friendships of others in high places. Favors were exchanged more frequently than those in the lower echelon knew about or could even imagine. Blackwell, like Hardy, had come up through the ranks and was very highly thought of in Washington circles. While Baker's problem certainly wasn't a CIA issue, Hardy knew that Blackwell could probably point him to a former CIA operative who was in the market to make a few extra bucks.

Blackwell was a pensive man known for his patience and excellent analytical skills. He had broad shoulders and more than one scar on his lean body from various covert operations he participated in over the years. He had spent his time in the trenches, paid his dues and had the political savvy needed to slip into an administrative role as his body weakened. He wore stylish, black-rimmed glasses. They were accentuated by his salt and pepper hair that began appearing when he reached the downhill side of fifty. Blackwell sat back in his chair, interlocked the fingers of both hands and twirled his thumbs as he looked out his window at the frosty landscape and mulled over a few names that might fit the task Hardy had in mind. The name Jack Wilder bubbled to the top of the list. He had been a member of the CIA's elite covert Looking Glass group. He'd served time in the Army Special Forces and had taken part in several joint covert CIA operations. Wilder had recently been instrumental in uncovering an oil conspiracy orchestrated by a high ranking U.S. Senator with Presidential aspirations. Wilder left the agency following the death of a Celeste Windham, a woman in Houston he'd been in love with. She had been killed in a shoot out with another woman who'd stalked and shot Wilder nearly taking his life. Blackwell had been the one to deliver the news of Celeste's death to Wilder as he lay in the hospital recovering from the gunshot wounds that nearly killed him.

Chapter 4

Addison had made the decision to leave New Hampshire behind forever. She had given herself a mission, a mission to call attention to the chaos of guns out of control in a country run by political morons whose only interests were lining their own pockets and serving the needs of lobbyists and big money donors, all without regard for the constituency that elected them. They were politicians with no regard for the damage they were causing society. The first step in her mission was to reclaim her old life, the life she had before Morgan and Joey, the life of a killer. To make it work, she felt the need to totally erase her New Hampshire existence. She wasn't sure how her quest would end or even where it would start. She just knew she would never be able to return to her home in New Hampshire. That life was gone forever.

She retrieved a pair of night vision goggles, a Black Hawk military knife, a Barret M98B sniper rifle, a nine millimeter Beretta, $70,000 in cash and a variety of bogus passports, credit cards and drivers' licenses from the huge safe in the basement that sat next to Morgan's workbench. She'd told Morgan the safe had come with the house and she didn't have any idea what the combination was or what was inside. Too heavy to move, it had became a fixture in the basement that was handy to stack things on. Each time Morgan would bring up the subject of possibly getting it open, Addison quickly changed the subject. He died never knowing the contents of the safe.

The next step had been to find a car that closely matched the family Lexus. She found one for sale in Alfred, Maine, called the number, confirmed it was still available and took a bus the ninety miles north to Alfred. A dark grey sky followed the bus like a veil the entire distance. A few flakes of snow fell occasionally as a reminder that winter was still in full bloom. She took a cab to the address listed in the ad for the car where she was met by Frank Lee, a cheerful old gentleman with rosy cheeks and white hair. With a long white beard and a bigger belly Frank could've been Santa Clause. He wore faded jeans and a red flannel shirt. The jeans were spotted and smeared with what looked like oil paint. The old guy told her he'd taken up oil painting to try and fill his long, lonely days after his wife died. They'd been married 46 years. Addison smiled at the old guy and said, "Good for you, I know it must be hard."

"She passed away just over a year ago," he replied, as he walked her around to the side of the house where the car was parked behind an old Jeep Cherokee. "Don't need two cars anymore," he'd said with a heavy sigh. This one was Betty's. I never liked it very much, just couldn't part with it," he said as he softly ran his hand along the car fender. Now it's time though." Addison gave Frank $5,000 cash for the car. There was no need to haggle over price. Addison could tell the old gentleman had an emotional attachment to the car, yet he knew it was time to let it go. He went in to the house and returned with the keys and the title. "Take good care of her," he said as he handed the over the items. As she drove off, she glanced in the mirror and saw the kindly old gentleman wiping tears from his eyes.

Addison parked the newly purchased Lexus in the garage and switched the plates from her Lexus to the one she'd just purchased. She then retrieved the garden hose from the front yard and headed back into the house. She carried the hose to the basement where she cut off a six foot piece. She cut the six foot piece in half lengthwise creating a miniature six foot canal. She stuffed some of Joey's silly putty in each end and filled the hose with gasoline. She carefully slipped one end of the gas filled hose under the water heater. Then she lit a small votive candle and carefully set it in the opposite end of the hose, sticking it into the silly putty. She figured it would be about an hour before the candle made its way to the gasoline fuel source and spread to the water heater. She went upstairs, blew out the pilot light on the gas stove in the kitchen and turned on all the burners. She'd quickly packed everything in the old, family Lexus and drove off, leaving the duplicate Lexus in the garage. In a few more minutes her old life, the one she'd always wanted, would be gone forever. There was no turning back.

The explosion rocked a good portion of the small town. It had been seen for miles. The only thing left standing was the old rock fireplace. The garage had burned and collapsed on the barely recognizable

Lexus in the garage. Everyone feared the worst; there was no way anyone could have survived the fire and explosion. The entire town was in shock. There was a lot of discussion in beauty salons and barber shops about the poor woman who'd lost her husband and child and then her own life in such a tragic accident.

After two days of aimless driving through Pennsylvania, Ohio and Indiana, Addison found herself cruising through the Portage Park neighborhood of Chicago where she first spotted the drug dealer. She'd driven the first few hundred miles of her journey in a daze not really knowing where she was going or exactly what it was she was going to do. She didn't think she could cry anymore, but the grief and the tears came back as she'd driven through the cold black night, thinking about Morgan and Joey. The white lines of the highway were blurred by her tears. Patches of snow covered the vacant farmland on either side of the long desolate highway. Cars coming her way were few and far between. The emptiness of the passing countryside pushed her mind back to the emptiness in her life, a void deeper than the Grand Canyon.

Her discovery of the drug dealer was the boost she needed to push the grief out of her mind, and formulate a plan. She left Chicago with the drug dealer's gun on the seat next to her.

The overwhelming grief crept back into Addison's mind as she once again found herself on a long dark desolate highway. Each mile she drove and each tear she shed pushed her life with Morgan and Joey further and further away. It was just past three a.m. when she pulled into the deserted parking lot of an all night diner near Cicero, Illinois just off I-55. She dried her tears with a tissue as she leaned forward and looked at her tired face in the rear view mirror. Sad swollen eyes once filled with joy stared back at her. She took a deep breath and got out of the car.

An icy breeze pushed at her back as she opened the wide glass door to the diner. The glass in the door was cracked. The fracture started at the bottom and ran just over half way up the vertical length of the door. It stopped just under the OPEN sign that was attached to a small suction device on the back side of the glass. An ancient looking waitress sat at the counter drinking coffee and smoking a cigarette. She turned and looked up as Addison walked in. An overweight cook stood behind the pass-through between the kitchen and the counter, reading a newspaper. Two burly arms held the newspaper close to his face as he struggled to read the small print. A ship anchor tattoo adorned each of his massive forearms. He was wearing a stained white apron and a San Francisco Giants baseball cap. The waitress had a wrinkled face, not from age, but from smoking. She'd made an attempt to cover the wrinkles with makeup, but it wasn't working.

Addison took a seat in a booth next to the window that looked out onto the empty parking lot. She was the only customer in the diner. The place was old but fairly clean except for the thin cloud of cigarette smoke that hung in the air over the counter where the waitress was sitting. The wrinkled waitress got up and slowly walked to the opposite end of the counter where she retrieved a menu from the top of a stack that sat next to a very old cash register.

"Here you go hon," the waitress said as she plopped the menu down in front of Addison, "Back in a second." She walked back to the counter, took a sip of coffee and a drag off the cigarette she'd left burning in the ashtray. She returned to the booth, took an order pad and pen out of her apron pocket. "So, what'll it be?" she said, as her nicotine stained fingers held the cheap ball point pen at the ready.

Addison couldn't remember the last time she'd eaten anything. Suddenly she was starving. She ordered a cheeseburger, fries and a cup of coffee. The hunger intensified as she smelled the burger and fries cooking in the kitchen. She inhaled the meal when it came, then ordered a piece of pecan pie topped with ice cream. She finished eating, had two more cups of coffee, stood and dropped a twenty on the table as she headed for the door. The waitress was back at her smoking station and the cook had his nose pushed deep into the newspaper. Neither of them looked up when she left.

She'd driven about ten miles after leaving the diner when she felt the bump. It came from the back of the car. The unmistakable slap, slap, slap of rubber hitting the pavement and the wheel well of the car came next. Addison pulled to the shoulder, got out and popped the trunk open. As she was looking for the spare, an eighteen wheeler pulled onto the shoulder and parked behind her. She was partially blinded by the big rig's headlights as the truck pulled up. She heard the hissing of air as the driver set the brake, turned his parking lights on and climbed down from the huge cab. He was a big guy, wearing a dark blue plaid flannel shirt, greasy jeans and scuffed work boots. He had a heavy beard and shaggy long hair that stuck out beneath a John Deere hat.

"Well, little Missy, looks like you could use some help," he said as he stood behind her and peered over her shoulder, his beard brushing the side of her face. She could smell alcohol and onions on his breath. "And you smell good too," he said as he put his huge arm around her left shoulder.

"No, thanks, I think I can handle it," she replied as she tried to step away from the odiferous trucker.

"Naw, better let me help," he said. "Let's put you in the sleeper of the truck where it's warm and we can talk about it." Still standing behind her, he pulled her close, wrapped his huge arms around her and lifted her off the ground pinning her arms against her body. He carried her to the passenger side of the truck, away from the prying eyes of passing cars. She knew in an instant what he had in mind and it sure as hell wasn't changing a flat tire. He lowered her feet to the ground and grabbed her breasts with his huge hands giving her just the opening she needed. She reached up pushing the palms of her hands into each of the brute's elbows breaking his hold. She spun and slammed her knee into his groin. His eyes opened wide as he gasped and bent forward in pain. The palm of her right hand crashed into the bottom of his nose adding to his misery. She could feel the cartilage crumble as his nose folded back onto his head. He fell to his knees, clutching his crotch with both hands; a steady stream of blood flowing from his shattered snout. She took two steps back to gain momentum, then two steps forward like a place kicker going for a field goal. She landed the kick dead center in the truck driver's side, pushing him into the small ditch next to the highway. He lay there moaning, unable to move, a broken nose and two cracked ribs.

Addison went back to the Lexus and finished changing the tire. She tossed the blown tire into the trunk of the Lexus and retrieved the Black Hawk knife from her duffle bag. She walked over to the driver and squatted down in the ditch next to him checking to make sure he was still breathing. His eyes widened with terror as she touched the knife to the side of his face and smiled. She pulled the trucker's cell phone out of his breast pocket, stood and walked back to his rig. With the precision of a surgeon she quickly plunged the military knife into the first of the eighteen tires. Less than five minutes later the huge Kenworth semi sat alongside the highway with eighteen flat tires. She returned the knife to the duffle bag in the trunk, opened the driver's phone and dialed 911. "There's a truck driver lying in a ditch on I-55 about ten miles south of Cicero," she said to the operator, "Looks like he may be having some serious trouble." She put the car in gear, tossed the cell phone out the window and drove off into the night.

Chapter 5

Addison headed south on I-55, jogged a few miles southwest and jumped on highway 53 towards Joliet, home of the famous prison that housed serial killer John Wayne Gacy for a short period. Gacy had been convicted of thirty-three murders that took place in Chicago between 1972 and 1978. The prison also once held the famous duo of Leopold and Loeb, two wealthy University of Chicago students convicted of kidnapping and killing fourteen year old Bobby Franks as they attempted to get away with the perfect crime. The two killers were defended by Clarence Darrow who was able to get a life sentence for the killers sparing them from the death penalty. Loeb was killed while at Joliet by a fellow inmate. After his release in 1958, Leopold migrated to Puerto Rico where he died of a heart attack in 1971. The famed prison had been open for business from 1858 to 2002.

After cruising past the prison, Addison took I-80 west. She was beginning to feel the effects of the long drive and beating up on truck drivers and drug dealers. She had been out of the game for a long time and her body was feeling the strain of it all. She took the exit marked Ladd, driving past a strip mall, a porn shop, a liquor store and a couple of service stations. She found a dilapidated looking motel and pulled in to register. The sign out front said "Frontier Mote, the neon "l" wasn't working on this particular night. The place was a dive, but she had stayed in worse places.

She was greeted at the front desk by a tall lanky East Indian whose name tag read "Vineet." He had a small black goatee and a huge black mole above his left eye. His wide smile showed a definite need for some serious dental work. She paid cash for the room and registered as Susan B. Anthony, knowing she wouldn't be asked for any identification. On the registration form she filled in the car make and model as a 1998 Chevy Blazer from Texas and made up a plate number on the spot. She parked the Lexus on the back side of the motel where it couldn't be seen and carried her things to her dingy room. A lamp with a broken shade sat on the bedside table and the bed was covered with an old tattered bedspread right out of the 1950's. She placed a chair beneath the door knob for a little extra security as she closed the door.

She took the drug dealer's gun out of the duffle and looked it over. It was a pretty beat up model 856 Tarus with a stainless steel barrel and cylinder that held six .38 caliber bullets. Still, the action and balance of the weapon fit her hand nicely. Oddly, the serial number was still intact on the weapon which most likely had been stolen from some affluent household in the Chicago area.

Addison laid the weapon aside and picked up the satchel containing her cash and various ID's. She pulled out a newspaper article she had cut out of the Wilson Bee, the day before she left New Hampshire. The article was about two Colorado State Legislators who had been recalled in a special election. The two democrats had provided critical support for strict gun control laws that had been passed by the State Legislature. The laws required background checks for private gun sales and limited ammunition magazines to no more that fifteen rounds. The National Rifle Association had poured buckets of money into ousting the two democrats. When she'd first read the article she wasn't sure why it had caught her attention, but she knew she needed to keep it. As she re-read it now an idea began to form in her mind.

The Colorado voice and driving force behind the recall was Burton T. Caldwell, a very wealthy man who owned twelve luxury car dealerships located throughout the state. A staunch conservative, Caldwell constantly used the second amendment to promote his cause. "As American citizens we have the right to keep and bear arms, blah, blah, blah." He was never without his trusty Beretta, housed in a shoulder holster which he always wore. It was prominently displayed under his left arm in every meeting he had with his employees. Some of them joked that he probably wore it in the shower.

Addison laid everything on the floor of the shabby motel room. She took her own Beretta out of her duffle, jacked a round into the chamber and set it on the bedside table next to the lamp. Despite her state of near exhaustion, sleep didn't come easy. She had a fitful night of near constant tossing and turning. Every time she drifted off to sleep she would see Morgan or Joey. First it was Morgan pushing Joey on the tire swing in the front yard. Then it was Morgan on his hands and knees sanding the kitchen floor, looking up at her with that devilish smile. The last image was the smile Joey gave her as he turned and blew her a kiss from the top of the steps on that last day of school. Joey's smiling face was replaced by a haunting vision of the failed mission in the Middle East. She was floating near the ceiling of a hospital room looking down at herself lying on her back in a hospital bed. Her eyes were nearly swollen shut and her face was covered in small lacerations caked over with dried blood. There was a tube of some sort in her mouth and intravenous lines ran out of both arms held in place by huge bandages. She looked closer and saw that both arms and legs were secured to the bedsides with leather straps. In the corner of the room she saw a man wearing a turban holding a rocket propelled grenade launcher. He smiled as he held the RPG in his arms and pointed it at the bed. From her floating position Addison tried to scream out and warn the figure in the bed but nothing came out of her mouth. The figure in the bed awoke with a frantic look in her eyes and started to twist and turn trying to free herself. The man in the turban laughed as he pulled the trigger. The bed became a smoldering twisted mass of metal and blood. The gruesome image slowly dissolved into nothing as the dream ended.

It was just past four-thirty in the morning when she gave up trying to sleep. She took a shower and put on a pair of worn jeans and an old sweatshirt. Still tired but at least clean and slightly refreshed she consulted a road atlas and set the Lexus on a course to Colorado.

Chapter 6

Jack Wilder sat on the tattered couch in the living room of his sparse Virginia apartment. He stared at the half empty bottle of Crown Royal on the coffee table next to the full clip for his Walther PPK .380 which he held in his right hand. He took another drink of Crown and picked up the clip as he sat the bottle down. The clip was loaded with hollow points to inflict the most damage possible. He popped the clip in the gun, jacked a round into the chamber and shoved the barrel up against his chin, had second thoughts, opened his mouth and placed the barrel against the roof of his mouth. This had become somewhat of a weekly ritual for the last six months. Usually at this point Jack's cat Angus would jump into his lap as if to persuade Jack to abandon his life ending plan. On this night however, Angus was nowhere to be found. Jack took the gun out of his mouth; leaned back and took one last look around.

The place was tastefully decorated in early Goodwill. Up until a year ago Wilder spent most of his time working on covert assignments all around the globe and never felt the need for fine furnishings. He had been a member of a CIA group called Looking Glass, an off-the-books black ops group that specialized in around-the-world problem solving for the U.S. It was the kind of problem solving that often would result in the demise of various brutal dictators or war lords. It was the kind of group that while loosely sanctioned by the government, those who were caught would quickly be disavowed and branded as rogue operatives acting on their own. It was the perfect balance of justice and corruption not unlike Congress itself except the latter weighed heavily on the corrupt side of the equation.

Two end tables that didn't match adorned either end of the derelict couch that held Wilder's inebriated frame. A coffee table made of knotty pine sat in front of the couch. It had been a three dollar bargain from the Goodwill store. In addition to the bottle of Crown, a half full bottle of Corona sat on the stained coffee table next to a small bowl, also half full of beer. The beer bowl belonged to Angus. Jack and the cat had been drinking buddies for several years now. The cat had come in through an open door one night when Jack returned from an assignment. The critter jumped up on the couch like he belonged there and had been a resident from that day forward. Jack and Angus had a connection, a camaraderie that was uncanny. They somehow seemed to understand one another.

Wilder was average in physical stature, an attribute that made it easy to blend in when he was working a covert operation. He had brackish brown hair and blue eyes. He was good looking by most standards but definitely not the type you'd see modeling clothes in GQ magazine. Nothing about him stood out that would give the average person reason to pay any attention to him. He was a trim one-eighty and stood just over five-ten. At forty-one he was physically fit and could run five miles with little effort or at least he had been able to six months earlier. He had served time in the Army Special Forces and had taken part in joint covert CIA-Special Forces operations a number of times. It was a natural fit when the CIA recruited him away from Special Forces and into the elite Looking Glass unit.

After several years at the agency Jack became disillusioned at the constant CYA attitude that had evolved. Paranoia about Congress kept getting in the way of getting things done, important things. In addition, there was little to no cooperation between the various agencies charged with protecting the United States. He'd finally had enough and was ready to leave the agency when his boss Alan Blackwell steered him to the Looking Glass group. There was no CYA attitude, no Congressional oversight to deal with. The only thing that mattered was getting the job done. There were no worries about legal parameters or constitutional rights to get in the way. The downside was being discovered, which meant being disavowed and erased from the CIA system like you never existed. For Jack, it had been a risk well worth taking.

Jack left the agency just over six months earlier after a series of tragic events had pushed him to the brink. He had been assigned to look into the assassination of a high level OPEC analyst in Vienna. The case led him to Houston, Texas where he rekindled an on again off again relationship with Celeste Windham, an old flame he had met at his best friend's wedding. At her insistence, Jack taught her how to shoot. She had spent countless hours at the shooting range and had become quite the marksman. Jack had been in the parking lot of Celeste's apartment when a deranged woman, who happened to be the widow of his best friend, put two bullets into him and was about to finish the job by putting one in his head as he lay bleeding on the pavement. Celeste witnessed the shooting from the front door of her apartment, drew her weapon and killed the crazed woman. The lunatic was able to get off one wild shot towards Celeste as she went down. It was one of those one in a million shots. The bullet pierced Celeste's heart and she died instantly. Jack had no idea what had happened until his former boss visited him in the hospital and gave him the bad news. He was devastated; he'd grown to love Celeste but had never actually told her so. He was wracked with guilt and grief over her death and blamed himself. Jack never found out who killed the OPEC analyst, but he did manage to put a U.S. Senator behind bars for orchestrating the assassination of the analyst. Soon after that, miserable and consumed with grief, Jack left the CIA for good. His days were filled with excessive drinking and zoning out on the couch in front of the television staying pretty oblivious to what was going on in the world around him. And now here he was, sitting on the couch building up the courage to put the gun in his mouth and end it all.

He closed his eyes ready to pull the trigger when he heard a familiar voice. He opened his eyes and there she was standing in the middle of the room staring at him. It was Celeste, or at least a vision of

42

Celeste. He could clearly see the hole in her chest from the bullet that killed her.

"Enough," she said. "You're being a coward and trying to take the easy way out. I really expected better of you, Jack Wilder." He blinked his eyes and looked around the dimly lit room. Was she really there or was he dreaming? As he leaned forward, her body slowly dissolved into a mist and vanished. Jack stood up, laid the gun on the couch and went into the bathroom and splashed cold water on his face. He stared at the miserable, gloomy image in the mirror. Bags the size of footballs clung to the bottom of his bloodshot eyes. Disheveled hair and two months of beard growth stared back at him. Angus reappeared and wove himself in and out of Jack's legs as Jack continued to stare at his pitiful self in the mirror. He didn't know if she was really there or not, but deep down he knew she was right. He had to stop feeling sorry for himself and get on with his life. He went to the coffee table, picked up what was left of the whiskey and poured it down the kitchen sink. He took a shower and went to bed. Angus ambled back to the living room, jumped up on the coffee table and finished his beer.

Early the next evening Jack sat on his couch mindlessly staring at the TV and the half full beer bottle on the coffee table trying to decide the next step in his life. He knew he had to change something but was struggling trying to think of the next step. At that moment his cell phone rang. He looked at the caller id and saw that it was a blocked number and almost didn't answer. Jeopardy had just switched to a commercial. *Ah, what the hell*, Jack thought as he muted the TV and answered the call.

"Jack, Alan Blackwell."

Jack blinked his eyes and shook his head trying to clear the cobwebs out of his addled brain. "Hey Alan, what's up?" He said as he stifled a yawn.

"A couple of things. First, just checking to see how you're doing these days and second, to see if you might have an interest in a little work."

"Well," Jack said as he leaned over, poured some of the half full beer bottle into the cat's dish and took a deep breath. "I'm taking it a day at a time. I'm sleeping a little better. No, that's a lie. I hardly sleep at all. Overall I guess there are good days and bad days, mostly bad."

"Maybe having something to do will help."

"Hmm, I don't think so Alan, I want to stay as far away from my former life as I possibly can."

"I understand, but just hear me out before saying no, ok? Do you know Bill Hardy over at the U.S. Marshal's Office?"

"Sure, wasn't he one of the brothers in mystery books written for teenagers back in the fifties?"

"Still a smart ass," Blackwell replied as he leaned back in his chair and picked out a spot on the ceiling to stare at. "That's a good sign. Actually he's the top dog in the U. S. Marshal's office. Those guys are the ones who, among other things, keep the Supreme Court Justices safe from the bad guys in the world."

"You're kidding; I thought you and your people got rid of all the bad guys left in the world?"

"Yeah right, I think there may be one or two left. Anyway, one of the Supreme Court Justices, Harold Baker, has been getting some pretty serious death threats and the Marshals don't have the staff to look into it. I thought you might have an interest in doing it. The money is great and it could be fun." Blackwell spotted a small spider slowly creeping across the ceiling headed for a wall. *Probably one of those spiders trained by the Russians to spy on the CIA.*

"I don't know Alan," Jack said as he got off the couch and headed to the kitchen in search of coffee. "I mean, I'm starting to become a pretty serious fan of Jeopardy and Wheel of Fortune. Do you think the good judge would give me time off to watch Alex and Pat?"

"That would be between you and his honor. I'll tell Hardy you'll stop by and see him sometime tomorrow. He'll give you the particulars on Baker. Oh and Jack, thanks, I owe you one." Blackwell rang off without waiting for a definite answer. He knew

Wilder well enough and was sure the former CIA operative would get in touch with Hardy.

Chapter 7

Wilder headed out to meet with Hardy early the next morning. He was met by the man's executive assistant and offered coffee which he gladly accepted before being ushered into the Director's office. He asked the Marshal to show him all the death threats that had come to Baker. To Jack's amazement Hardy handed him a folder containing fifty-three death threats that had been mailed to the Supreme Court Justice. "These are the ones for the last six months," Hardy said as he handed them to Jack and took a sip of his coffee.

"Wow, I'll bet Madonna doesn't get this much fan mail."

"Can't tell you much about Madonna unless she's in the witness protection program," Hardy said with a chuckle. "Actually, I couldn't tell you anything about her if she was in the witness protection program."

Jack took a seat at a table in the corner of Hardy's office and began reading through the Judge's mail carefully studying each line of every letter in between sips of coffee. He sat four of the letters aside and asked for copies that he could take with him. "With these four exceptions it looks like the majority of are probably from harmless crack pots who couldn't find their ass with both hands" he said, pointing to the letters he'd set aside. "All four have an Oregon postmark and probably came from the same person or persons." Hardy summoned an assistant who took the letters and came back with the requested copies and a coffee pot to freshen Jack's cup. Jack folded the letters and tucked them into his coat pocket. He thanked Hardy for his hospitality and headed to D.C. to see the Honorable Harold Baker.

Jack turned up the collar of his jacket to ward off a cold northerly wind that was rapidly pushing snow filled clouds into what had been a pale blue sky only two hours earlier. He set his Styrofoam coffee cup in the console between the bucket seats of his BMW Z4 roadster as he slid into the seat. While he was frugal in his living accommodations, he was extravagant when it came to his personal transportation. The crimson red rocket had set him back just over fifty thousand but he felt it was worth every penny.

He pulled out his cell phone and dialed Barry Godley as he waited for the car to warm up. Godley was a research analyst at the CIA who sucked up high octane caffeine energy drinks like there was no tomorrow. He was also a computer whiz of the highest degree. Barry was the quintessential computer nerd if ever there were one. He wore a short sleeve plaid shirt that held a pocket protector stuffed with various colored pens and pencils which he rarely used. Most of the time his hands and fingers were busy flying all over his keyboard, which always had a high octane energy drink parked nearby. His thick, black rimmed glasses were tucked in under his long, unruly hair which framed a long acne scarred face with slightly oversized lips. His best feature besides his incredible brain was his eyes. He did have deep blue eyes that would be the envy of any movie star. He wore stained khaki pants that were too short for his thirty-three inch inseam. White socks and black shoes completed the look which lent credence to the "computer nerd" label he'd been given by his CIA associates long ago. "Barry the Wonder Boy," they called him. He was a strict vegan, a hair short of six feet tall and skinny as a rail.

"Barry, Jack Wilder here."

"Jack! What's up Spymaster? How are you? Where are you? Where have you been? They said you quit, vamoosed, skedaddled, rode off into the sunset never to be seen again. Tell me it ain't true, Jackie boy. Tell me you were just kidnapped by aliens and they just sent you back because they couldn't figure you out."

"Barry, you gotta quit drinking that stuff. One of these days your heart is going to be pumping so fast it's going to explode," Jack said as he put the Beamer in gear and pulled out of the parking lot.

"No can do Jack, it's what keeps me going. Know what I mean? It's my whole reason for living. Well that and my girlfriend. You remember Fiona don't you, my dreamboat, my soul mate, the love of my life, my one true goddess who keeps me sane and on track? So, what can I do for you old pal of mine?

Jack took a sip of his rapidly cooling coffee while Barry took a huge gulp of his energy drink and promptly belched into the phone.

"Well Barry, it's true, I did quit. I'm a free agent waiting for the right opportunity to come along. In the meantime I'm just picking up odds and ends which brings me to the point of this call; I have a favor to ask."

"Anything for you my brother, just ask and you shall receive."

"I need you to dig up everything you can find on Harold Baker; he's a Supreme Court Justice."

"I can do that. How soon do you need it?"

"No hurry, a couple of hours will do."

"Ha, call you back in half an hour," the Wonder Boy replied. With that the line went dead and Barry started punching keys on his keyboard.

A light snow began to fall accompanied by the usual chaotic traffic as Jack slowly began the trek into D.C. He was just crossing the Roosevelt Memorial Bridge in the slow moving bumper to bumper traffic, made even slower by the falling snow when all movement stopped. He craned his neck to the left to see two cars sitting perpendicular to the traffic flow in the middle of the bridge. Both drivers were out and yelling at each other, their heads turning white from the snow. One was a new Cadillac of some kind and the other appeared to be a Lexus. ZZ Top's "La Grange" was blasting through the speakers of Jack's high end car stereo system. He cranked the volume even higher and sat back to wait for traffic to clear which wouldn't be anytime soon. At about two minutes into ZZ Top, Jack's cell phone rang. It was Barry calling him back. Jack turned the volume down and answered. He could hear Barry singing a horrible impersonation of a Paul Simon song "Just slip out the back Jack, make a new plan Stan," as he answered. "Barry, don't give up your day job. You couldn't carry a tune in a bucket."

"Jack, you dog, you hurt my feelings. You know what a sensitive guy I am."

"So tell me, Mr. Sensitivity, what did you find out?"

"Ok, here's the scoop Dude: Baker grew up with a silver spoon in his mouth, has two brothers, dad who was a high powered attorney in Dallas and died a few years back. He left his widow and the three sons a huge, and I mean an extra large king size kind of huge, bucket of money. The good judge worked in daddy's firm, met all the right political people, rose quickly through the judicial ranks and sailed through each hearing confirmation in record time. He married his Yale law school sweetheart, still married, never had kids and the guy is a rabid conservative republican. He's anti-abortion, pro guns, thinks global warming is a sham and always sides with the most

51

conservative of his colleagues on the bench. He and the Mrs. live in a refurbished Victorian over in Georgetown that they paid just over three mil for. That's like three million in cash American green backs. Oh, and he likes coffee, loves it in fact. He recently purchased a fancy new Jura Impressa Z7 espresso maker for $2,163.49.

"Barry, how in the hell did you know the exact, never mind, I don't even want to know. Thanks kid, I'll have a case of that high octane lemonade sent over to you when I get a chance."

"No problemo Jackie boy, call anytime."

During his conversation with Barry, Jack had crept up all of two car lengths. The vehicles ahead of him found a narrow path around the crashed vehicles. He cautiously followed. As he passed the Caddy and the Lexus, the two drivers were still yelling and pointing at each other. It was a smooth drive the rest of the way to the Supreme Court building. The snow had eased up a bit and the slow moving traffic seemed to have melted some of the snow on the road.

The Supreme Court building located on First St. NE is a massive four story neoclassical structure that was completed in 1935. The 24 columns making up part of façade are made of marble imported from the Montarrenti quarries near Siena, Italy. The building's architect, Cass Gilbert petitioned then Italian Premier Benito Mussolini to guarantee that only the highest quality marble be made available for the project.

As Jack cruised past the west side of the building he noticed the inscription on the building "equal justice under the law." *More equal to some than others, depending on how much money you have,* Jack muttered to himself as he searched for a parking spot. He found a decent place on Maryland Avenue and hiked through the cold, lightly falling snow the long block back to the building. He walked past a group of tourists bundled up in heavy overcoats, hats and gloves. They were holding a soggy map trying to get their bearings. "The hell with this, let's just find the closest coffee shop and get warm," he heard one of them say as he walked past the group. A few steps later he came upon a homeless man sitting on a bench and shivering badly. Jack took a ten out of his wallet and handed it to the guy. "Here pal, go find a warm spot in a restaurant and buy yourself a bowl of soup." He wondered what the story was behind the guy on the bench. *What is it in life that puts a person on such a path?* He couldn't help but wonder if the past six months of his own life weren't perhaps a preview of that kind of a path.

Jack entered the Supreme Court Building through the ground level doors located on the plaza side of the building. He was greeted by a uniformed guard, a metal detector and an x-ray machine. He gave his name to the guard and showed the man his id. The guard did a quick check to find Jack's name on a list attached to a clipboard. The burly guard pointed to a bench against the wall past the x-ray machine. "Have a seat over there and someone from the Court will be down to escort you up shortly." Jack took a seat and watched as a parade of lawyers, clerks and administrators put their briefcases, purses and laptops on a conveyor belt that went through the x-ray machine. They then joined the queue to go through the metal detector. It was easy to tell who the lawyers were. They were all wearing gray suits, white shirts, red ties and gray or black overcoats. Jack thought there must be a class in law school on how to dress to look like the other guy. He'd once heard a joke about an old priest on his death bed who summoned his lawyer and his banker to be with him in his final moments. The banker asked the old man why he'd chosen the two of them out of the entire congregation to be with him at this time. The old priest looked at each of them then replied, "I want to die like Jesus did, with a thief on either side of me." Jack chuckled to himself as he recalled the joke.

"Mr. Wilder," Jack looked up to see a tall, lean redhead dressed in dark green slacks and a yellow blouse. She looked like a marathon runner or perhaps a swimmer. "I'm Jeanne Nichols, Justice Baker's personal secretary," the attractive woman said as she held out her hand.

"Nice to meet you," Jack said as he stood and shook her hand.

"Follow me please. Justice Baker will be in his chambers shortly."

"So have you been with His Honor very long?" Jack asked as they bypassed the security area all together and headed up a stairway.

"Yes, nearly 12 years. I was actually his paralegal back in Texas when he worked in his father's law firm. He has taken me with him through each of his court appointments. I never had an interest in being married or having a family, so it's worked out very well for me, for both of us actually. I think he is probably the hardest working member of the Supreme Court. A twelve hour day for him is not at all unusual."

"Do you know anything about the death threats he seems to be getting with some regularity?"

"Not really, he keeps that stuff pretty much to himself. I have seen a few that have come here to his office since opening his mail is one of my responsibilities. For some reason a lot of them have gone directly to his home, which is odd because home addresses of Supreme Court members are kept pretty confidential."

They entered a tastefully decorated reception area just outside Baker's office. The dark walnut paneling held a variety of pictures of the Justice posing with all of Washington's elite and a few assorted military people, mostly Generals and an Admiral or two. Also included were pictures of Baker with the Presidents Bush and other high ranking republican politicos.

"Would you care for coffee or tea while you wait? Justice Baker should be down shortly. He is just finishing up his weekly three-on- three basketball game on the fifth floor. He is proud of the fact that his team usually wins. I don't think it's a coincidence that he always finds law clerks who are former basketball players and nearly always over six foot to play on his side."

"Coffee would be nice, thanks very much." Nichols stepped through a side door and returned in less than a minute with a silver tray tastefully set with a coffee carafe, a pitcher of cream, a sugar bowl and two elegant china coffee cups with matching saucers.

Jack had just poured himself a cup from the coffee service when Baker walked in. He was dressed in a Nike warm up outfit and wearing an expensive pair of Air Jordan shoes. "I see that Jeanne has taken good care of you," Baker said as he held out his hand. Let's go into my chambers and visit shall we?" Baker pointed to the door on the left.

The man's office was not at all what Jack had expected. He figured there would be stacks of papers and law books covering every inch of a huge desk and files of legal briefs scattered about the room. Instead he found a neat, well organized and tastefully decorated office space. The décor included a variety of original oil paintings and a smattering of bronze works by an artist he didn't recognize. It was a cavernous space with ten foot ceilings and dark wood paneling on every wall. The East wall was covered with large windows that looked out on the busy streets of Washington. An oversized walnut desk and credenza took up one side of the huge space. The desktop held a leather blotter, a few files, an ornate Tiffany desk lamp and a large gold framed picture of Mrs. Baker. Behind the desk was an expensive high backed cordovan leather chair trimmed in a walnut that matched the desk. A stately American flag stood sentry in the corner of the room behind the desk. Opposite the desk were two wingbacked leather chairs. A large leather couch, a glass-topped coffee table and two more of the high backed leather chairs made up a cozy sitting area in one corner or the large office. Baker followed Jack in carrying the coffee service tray which he set on the glass coffee table. He poured himself a cup and motioned for Jack to take a seat.

"So, Mr. Wilder, you come highly recommended. But, before we get into specifics, let me ask you a question. In the grand scheme of things do you consider yourself a liberal or a conservative?"

"Really neither," Jack replied. "I'm just a poor former public servant trying to eke out a living like most Americans. I think that well over ninety percent of Congress is made up of crooks and shysters who are totally out of touch with the people who elected them. They're bought and paid for by lobbyists and other outside interests. Representing the American people is a totally foreign concept to them. On the other hand when it comes to protecting a Supreme Court Justice I'm pretty conservative about keeping losses to a minimum. And when it comes to using bullets to protect a Justice, well, I'm pretty liberal with the number I use."

"Well, I'll take that as a subtle way of you telling me it's none of my business, and that's the way it should be. I don't want somebody protecting me who only tells me what I want to hear. I want someone who will tell me to shut up and duck when that's what needs to be done." Jack took a sip of his coffee and casually looked around the room. The walls all seemed to exude an aura of power and prestige. He looked back at Baker and pulled one of the death threats out of his pocket and laid it on the table between them. "Tell me, your Honor, what do you make of this particular letter?" Jack said. A picture of Baker's younger brother and his wife was printed at the top of the page. Beneath the picture were the words "we're coming for them, then you."

"Well, I have to say it's certainly one of the most disturbing threats I've ever received. A threat against me is one thing but when they bring my family into it that's really crossing the line." Baker took another sip of coffee, furled his brow and leaned back in his chair as he looked across the table at Jack. "So, Mr. Former Public Servant, tell me, what's our next step?"

"Well, I think the most prudent thing to do would be to ask your brother and his family to take a vacation for a week or two and the sooner the better. That will give me time to do some checking on who these bozos might be and what they're up to. If they're after your brother and his family, I need to find them before they can do anything." Jack took a sip of his coffee and stood to leave. "I've always wanted to see the Pacific Northwest," he said. "I'm going to start by going to Eugene to see what I can dig up. In the meantime you have my number. Please don't hesitate to give me a call if anything new crops up. I'll be back in touch in a couple of days." He shook hands with Baker and headed out. Baker picked up the phone and called his brother and explained the situation. His brother agreed to send his wife to her mother's in Texas for a week or so but he refused to commit to going with her. "Too many customers to take care of and lots to do," he said.

The snow had stopped and the gray clouds were beginning to part, but the temperature had dropped considerably as Jack made the cold trek back to his car. As soon as he got back in his car and got the heater going, he hit the speed dial button on his cell phone for Barry the CIA whiz kid. "Barry, buddy, I have another favor to ask."

"Anything Jack, you name it and my keen mind and surprisingly quick nimble fingers can find it."

"I need you to dig up a list of all the do-good-radical groups located in the Eugene, Oregon area. I think one of them may be sending threatening letters to one of our esteemed Supreme Court Justices."

"No problem my fine former spy friend, I'll have a list to you in the next half hour or so."

"Thanks kid." Jack hung up and pulled into the rush hour traffic. Oddly, the clouds had closed back up and the snow began to fall again. This time the temperature had dropped enough for the flakes to freeze as they hit the busy street causing traffic to move at the pace of an overweight turtle with arthritis. Jack hated driving his sport BMW in winter traffic. As h cautiously drove home, he decided that when he had time he would purchase an old Junker four wheel drive of some sort to drive in bad weather conditions, which seemed to be more and more frequent these days.

Jack had just put the key in the lock to his apartment door when Wonder Boy called back. "So tell me Kid, what did you find out?" he said as he opened the door.

"Well, for starters, Eugene is one weird town. Did you know they have some kind of festival/parade thing every year down there, or up there, wherever the heck it is and the Queen of the shindig is called, are you ready for this, the Slug Queen. We're not talking something like a Prom Queen here Jack. I Googled slugs. Not pretty, not pretty at all. They're slimy little leech worm snail looking things with antennae, disgusting little creatures. Whoever the Queen of the party is she's got to be one ugly woman."

Jack stepped inside where he was met by Angus with his usual scowl. Jack kicked off his shoes, grabbed a beer from the fridge, plopped down on the couch and put his feet up on the wobbly coffee table. Angus jumped up on the table and rubbed his head against Jack's feet waiting expectantly for Jack to share his beer. "Ok, so thanks for the Chamber of Commerce sales pitch, but what did you find out about radical groups?"

"Oh, right, radical groups. Well, they have a group for just about everything. There's the anti pesticide group, the homeless advocate group, the free Tibet group, and then there's the CREEPs."

"The creeps?" I thought they were some kind of gang."

"No Jack, that's the Crips, you know, East LA, the Crips and the Bloods? That kind of stuff."

"Oh," Jack said as he poured some of his beer into Angus' drinking bowl. So tell me about these creeps."

"CREEPs stands for Citizens for Responsible Environment and Energy Protection. I also looked up all the Supreme Court cases dealing with energy and environment. Baker voted in favor of pillaging the land and energy resources every time. I'm thinking if someone in Weirdsville is sending letters to Baker with the fancy coffee maker, it's one of these creeps from CREEPs."

"Ok, thanks Barry, I owe you yet another one, just put it on my tab. One of these days I'll take you and your girlfriend out for a nice expensive dinner somewhere."

Jack hung up the phone and ran his hand over Angus' head. The cat stopped slurping long enough to look up at Jack and burp before turning back to his evening libation.

Chapter 8

George Franklin was livid as he walked up the steps into his luxurious Gulf Stream G650. The streamlined luxury jet had set him back a cool sixty five million but was well worth the price. He had huge construction projects going on all over the globe. This particular project was over budget and two months behind. He wasn't sure who he would get to finish it but there was always someone available when the right amount of cash was waved at them. He had just fired the construction manager and his top two assistants. They all had families to support and the overruns really weren't their fault. The timeline expectations were totally unrealistic as was the budget but Franklin didn't care. He wanted results not excuses. As he reached the top step of the gangway into the opulently furnished jet it hit him, a chest pain so intense it took his breath away. He reached for the railing as the pain shot down both his arms. He collapsed on the floor and rolled over onto his back gasping for breath as his face turned an ashen gray.

The jet's pilot made the 911 call and a half hour later the millionaire developer was being loaded into the back of an ambulance. His pain subsided when the EMT squirted a mist of nitro under his tongue on the way to the hospital. At the hospital he was made comfortable and punched full of IV's as blood was drawn and the docs started working on a diagnosis, "most likely a heart attack," Franklin heard one of them say.

George Franklin wasn't a billionaire, at least not yet. He was however a millionaire several times over. His net worth was estimated to be somewhere around eight-hundred million. This of course never stopped him from telling people he was a billionaire. He had this constant need for attention, a narcissistic personality some people called it. He was sixty-nine years old and hid his gray hair with a perpetual blondish dye job. He wore suits custom tailored to fit his portly frame. At just under five-ten, even with his custom made suits, his two hundred twenty-five pounds hung on his frame like ten pounds of potatoes in a seven pound bag. He rarely got any exercise and had a fondness for anything sweet. His basic food groups were caffeine, sugar and grease. His best features were his baby blue eyes tucked beneath his expensive Cary Grant glasses and his charismatic sociopathic personality. He was the kind of guy who could talk anybody into anything. Despite his plumpness he was one of the world's most eligible bachelors, but showed little interest in women. After two failed marriages that cost him just over a million dollars each and could have been worse if it hadn't been for the pre-nups he'd sworn off women. Instead he focused on his one true love other than himself, making money.

Originally from Texas he'd made his first twenty million in the oil business. As the oil business began to wane he bought television stations in what he thought were rapidly growing markets. Most of them turned out to be gold mines and returned a ten-fold profit when he sold them a few years later. His next step was real estate development. That's when his fortune really began to climb. He developed hotels and office buildings in big cities all over the world. All located in high rent districts. He also bought, refurbished and sold several resort properties cashing in on bankruptcies of previous resort developers. He was able to acquire bankrupt resorts for pennies on the dollar leaving previous owners gasping in his wake. He had a "take no prisoners" attitude and never felt any remorse for those he took advantage of as his fortune increased. Big business is a game played on a world stage in which there are winners and losers. George Franklin was a winner.

Franklin's holdings included luxury four star hotels in Dallas, Los Angeles, San Francisco, New York and Acapulco. In addition to his hotel and resort properties he owned several hundred thousand acres of pristine wilderness land in Montana, Wyoming, Colorado and Utah. The largest plot was just over 90,000 acres in Montana. It was land Franklin purchased from several cattle ranchers in the area after first purchasing the land holding the water that flowed to the ranchers' properties. A few of the ranchers tried to hold on but quickly realized the expense of trying to drill wells for water wouldn't provide the return they needed to survive in the cattle business.

Franklin woke to the voice of a nurse saying he had given the staff quite a scare. He had no recollection of being sleepy or falling asleep. He glanced over at the chair next to his bed. Lying on the chair was his undershirt that had been cut from the bottom to the neck. Then it dawned on him, he had checked out, died, and was brought back to life through the miracle of defibrillation. The nurse told him they had to shock him four times to get him back. There had been no warning, no discomfort of any kind. He was just here one second and gone the next. It was as if someone had flipped a switch and he was gone. That's when the panic set in. He realized just how fragile life really is. No matter how much money you have, you can still die at the drop of a hat. He knew people who had died, of course, but never thought of himself dying. And now here he was lying in that hospital bed staring at the ceiling struggling with his own mortality. And then it came to him. He'd been brought back for a reason. If he was going to hit the billion dollar mark he would need to work harder than ever. And why stop at a billion? Why not go for becoming the richest guy in the world? If life is that short and fragile you have to grab all you can while you're here. He became more determined than ever to crush his enemies and build the greatest financial empire in the world.

The next day he was paid a visit by Judd Collins of Collins, Hollingsworth and Sweeny. They were one of the biggest firms in D.C. and had the most experience of any firm in the field of real estate litigation. To Franklin's dismay after he fleeced the ranchers in Montana out of their land, he realized that through a stupid oversight of a now former employee, his company had failed to acquire the mineral. Those rights had been retained by the BLM when the various ranchers had originally purchased the land. The BLM subsequently leased those rights to a huge energy conglomerate known as Future Energy Exploration and Development Inc. Future Energy had served notice to Franklin of their intent to begin gas, oil and coal exploration on his 90,000 acres and the litigation battle had begun. A temporary injunction had been granted giving Franklin's people time to prepare their case. Three years and five million dollars in legal fees later, the case landed in the lap of the Supreme Court. Judd Collins had fought Future Energy through all the lower courts and had argued the case before the Supreme Court. Collins had argued the case eleven months earlier and the decision had come down at about the same time Franklin was rolling around on the floor of his Gulf Stream. The case on a 5- 4 vote had been ruled in Future Energy's favor. Despite his heart condition Franklin nearly exploded when Collins gave him the news. Harold Baker, the most conservative of the nine member judiciary voted to give Future Energy permission to destroy thousands of acres of pristine wilderness for energy exploration. That was thousands of acres Franklin had planned on developing into golf courses and luxurious high end housing developments.

Franklin was well acquainted with Justice Baker and his judicial arrogance. He had carefully researched each of the nine Justices when the case was put on the Supreme Court docket. He knew Baker's tendencies to always side with the government on any case that had come up. It was as if he was repaying those who had helped him reach his lofty perch on the Court. He'd anticipated a 5-4 vote but thought it was going to be in his favor. At the last minute one of the other judges who had been on the fence voted against him.

Franklin's sudden rise in blood pressure, despite the heavy medication, set off an alarm at the nurse's station. The head nurse came in, gave Franklin a shot to calm him down and ushered Collins out of the room.

Chapter 9

Brian Benavidez was sitting in his car on the top level of the Union Station parking garage on Massachusetts Avenue listening to the overture from La Traviata. It was 2 A.M. and Brian's $94,000 dark blue S-Class Mercedes was the only car in the entire structure. He was backed into the parking space to insure a clear view of approaching vehicles. He looked at his watch as the Senator's Mercedes pulled into the space next to his, right on time. The window came down on the driver's side of the Senator's car. The good Senator was alone, as instructed.

"Have you got the money?" Benavidez asked as he turned down the volume on the opera overture. The Senator gave him a disgusted look and handed him an envelope containing $50,000 in cash.

"And now, the pictures," the Senator snapped. Benavidez opened the briefcase on the passenger seat, took out a similar envelope and passed it across to the Senator. "This includes the negatives?" the Senator asked.

"Of course, no more worries Senator. I'll never trouble you again. It's been a pleasure doing business with you."

"The pleasure is all yours for sure you son-of-a-bitch," the Senator barked as he sped off into the night.

The Senator, of course didn't know about the second set of negatives. Being somewhat true to his word Benavidez really had no intention of using them, unless of course someday the Senator was to run for President. Who knew what the price for pictures of the married Senator with one of his young interns would be worth then? One could only imagine. Benavidez put the envelope in his inside coat pocket, gave it a loving pat and drove off.

Brian Benavidez is one of those Washington political low life sleaze bags known to every Senator and Congressman and used by many. He was never talked to, or about in open spaces where conversations could be overheard. Any discussion regarding the low profile crook was always done behind locked doors or on secure phone lines. He was a small man, just over five-six with dark brown beady eyes, a thin mustache and black hair which he combed straight back. He was the only child of Cuban immigrants who had fled Cuba for Miami during the early years of the Castro regime. His father had been a serious alcoholic and was stabbed to death in a bar fight in Miami when Brian was only ten-years old. His mother took a variety of domestic servant jobs and at one time worked for Donald Trump at his famous Mar-a-Lago resort. The job was short lived however. She and several others quit when one of their friends, a contractor who worked for the Trump organization, was never paid. After being stiffed by the famous billionaire he had to lay off several loyal employees and nearly went bankrupt.

After several scrapes with law enforcement Brian left home on his eighteenth birthday. He slipped out in the middle of the night while his mother slept. She woke to find a note taped the dresser mirror telling her not to worry. After several years of dealing with the juvenile justice system, compliments of her wayward son, she actually felt relieved. Brian worked his way across the U.S. doing odd jobs, most of which were illegal and eventually landed in Washington D.C., the world capital of corruption. It was there that he perfected the art of crashing political events. At first it was for the great food layouts these kinds of functions were known for. You merely needed to say you were a part time clerical worker in Senator so-and-so's office and people quickly left you alone in search of someone higher up the food chain to chat with; someone with whom favors could be exchanged as a means to personal career advancement. He eventually met and made friends with Senatorial aides and quickly learned how and where to look for the secrets that politicians want to keep hidden. It was a short step from there to blackmailing various political windbags for fun and profit.

Benavidez exuded an aura of a crooked horse jockey, the kind that would take a bribe or dope a horse without giving it a second thought. He was the guy you called to do something when you didn't want to get your hands dirty. If you wanted to start a nasty rumor about a political opponent Benavidez he would get it done. If you wanted pictures of a congressman going into a hotel room with an intern, Benavidez was your man. If you wanted someone totally erased, Benavidez could put you in touch with the right people. He had cataloged enough dirt over the years that his testimony or conversation with the right people could probably put two out of every five members of congress behind bars.

A year or so earlier, former Senator and current jailbird Hamilton Kingsbury III had been behind the assassination of an OPEC analyst in a bold effort to fix oil prices and set himself up for a run at the Presidency. Kingsbury was now doing time at a maximum security federal prison in Florence, Colorado, thanks to someone from his inner circle turning against him and providing the authorities with enough evidence to put him away for a long time. While Kingsbury had used his power and influence over the years to ruin hundreds of lives, he had never killed or had anyone killed until he decided he wanted to be President. As his greed for money and power pushed him towards the White House, he easily rationalized that sacrificing a human life was a small price to pay for becoming the leader of the free world. Kingsbury had one of his minions search for a way to get rid of the pesky OPEC analyst. It was Brian Benavidez who ultimately provided Kingsbury with the number to call to arrange for the hit on the analyst.

Benavidez had no qualms about putting people in touch with those who would kill for a fee. He was the classic textbook definition of a sociopathic disorder; he had antisocial attitudes and behaviors along with a total lack of conscience. In addition, he had that one quality essential for a sociopath to succeed, charisma. He could charm the socks of the Queen of England if the occasion called for it.

Chapter 10

George Franklin took a sip of his fifth glass of champagne and looked at his watch, willing the time to pass more quickly. It was only 8 o'clock. He figured he had at least one more hour of shaking hands and being cordial to a bunch of other rich people he didn't really know or care about before he could make an exit. He had only been out of the hospital for a month and this was the third fundraiser he had attended in as many weeks. He was still reeling from the disastrous Supreme Court decision that had cost him a fortune, yet here he was a some kind of money begging affair pledging to give away more of his wealth to some crooked politician. The only redeeming thing about the three events was that he had the opportunity to trash talk the honorable Harold Baker to anyone who would listen. With every person he met and every hand he shook he would start the conversation with, "So tell me, what do you think of Justice Harold Baker?" By the end of each conversation he was able to tell the other person what a miserable, no good son-of-a-bitch he thought Baker was.

When Brian Benavidez overheard millionaire George Franklin complaining about Justice Baker he could almost hear the whistle of the cash train headed his way. Benavidez followed the half drunk millionaire to the bar. "So, you would like to see that old buzzard Baker hit the road eh?" he said to Franklin.

"You damn right I would."

"They're appointed for life you know."

"Yeah, and that's part of the problem. The old buzzard isn't really all that old."

"Sometimes they just die, you know. Heart attack, get hit by a bus, an airplane crashes."

"Well, couldn't happen soon enough for me." Franklin said as he took a drink of his freshly poured champagne. "The guy is just no damn good for business and that's all there is to it."

Benavidez leaned closer to Franklin, glanced around to be sure no one was listening and whispered, "What would it be worth to you to see him gone?" "What?" Franklin responded. Benavidez leaned closer still, took a drink of his rum and Coke and said, "How badly would you like to see the guy go?" Benavidez reached past Franklin and picked up a bar napkin. He took a pen out of his pocket and wrote an address on it. He held the napkin up so Franklin could read the address then tore the napkin into tiny pieces. "Meet me at that address at 3:00 o'clock tomorrow afternoon." He turned and walked away tucking the napkin pieces into his coat pocket.

The sky was a dark gray and the temperature was in the mid-thirties the next afternoon when Franklin parked his car in front of the non-descript office building on Connecticut Avenue. He took the elevator to the fourth floor and knocked on the door marked 416. Benavidez opened the door and quickly closed it behind Franklin. The office space was nothing but an empty room, drab yellow walls and an old ugly beige carpet. "Take off your top coat and suit coat" Benavidez commanded. Franklin was somewhat taken aback but complied, looked around and dropped the coats on the floor. "Now, remove your tie and unbutton your shirt" Benavidez said.

"Now hold on there cowboy, just what the hell is going on?" Franklin responded, as he stiffened and took a step backwards.

"Mr. Franklin, you have come to me asking for help with a very complicated business matter, one that in fact may border on being illegal. If this conversation were to be recorded it could prove to be a disaster for both of us. These are simply precautions I take."

"Ah, that makes sense I guess" Franklin said as he unbuttoned his shirt.

"Ok" Benavidez said, satisfied that Franklin wasn't wearing a wire. "Here's what's going to happen. Meet me here again tomorrow at 3:00 again and bring an envelope with fifty thousand cash in it. Do not say anything, just knock. I will open the door, you will step in and I will give you a slip of paper with a phone number on it, you will then hand me the envelope, turn and walk out the door. At that point our business is concluded. You call the number and anything after that is between you and the man on the other end of the line. I won't know and don't want to know what happens after that. You can see yourself out."

The next day Franklin dropped off the cash, picked up the number and made the call. Darth Vader answered the phone, or at least someone using some kind of voice modulation device that sounded like Darth Vader. "Balstrop" was all the strange voice said. "Uh, hello, this is George Franklin calling. I got your number from…." "I know where you got the number" the voice on the other end interrupted. "I have been expecting your call. Write down this number." Franklin took down the number of a bank account in Switzerland. "Deposit one point five million U.S. dollars into that account in the next ten days and I'll have one of my associates start working on your problem. The problem should be gone sometime within the next 90 days after which time you have two days to deposit another one point five million into the same account. If that isn't done you will be dead in less than a month. Do you understand everything I have said?" Franklin swallowed hard and said "yes," then the line went dead. Three days later Franklin wired the money to the Swiss account as instructed.

Chapter 11

Two days and nearly a thousand miles later
Addison cruised through the small Colorado town of
Brighton, Colorado just off I-76 a little north of
Denver. The small town established in the 1870's had
been named after Brighton Beach, New York. She
drove through the old downtown area on Main Street
past a variety of antique shops, a barbershop and a
beauty parlor. Several women in the beauty parlor
were sitting in chairs under old style hair dryers
reading magazines.

Addison found a parking spot next to an old Ford
pick-up truck loaded with bales of hay. She got out of
the car, stood on her tiptoes and held her arms up
stretching out her back and arms. Her muscles were
tight from the long drive. She looked up at the pale
blue sky and watched a few lazy clouds push their
way toward the Rockies. The air was clear, clean and
cool. She took in a deep breath, held it for a few
seconds and exhaled as she finished her stretch. A
very old German Shepherd with a nearly white
muzzle was laying on one of the hay bales soaking up
the morning sunshine. The old dog stretched, stood on
its wobbly legs and walked expectantly to the edge of
the truck. Addison held the back of her hand under
the dog's nose as she took a step closer to the truck.
The dog sniffed Addison's hand and put its head
down looking for a scratch between the ears. Addison
obliged and saw the dog's name on its collar tag,
Lena. "You're a good old girl Lena," Addison said as

she scratched the dog's head. "I'll bet you brought a lot of love and pleasure to a family in your time." She softly patted the Shepherd on the head as she pictured the dog in its prime, chasing kids around a big yard or perhaps retrieving a ball and joyfully running it back to her owner. Addison gave the dog one last pat and went into the store wondering how many years the old gal had left.

An old bell attached to a spring at the top of the door jingled as Addison made her way into the wig shop next to the beauty parlor. A young woman with an overly abundant bust line wearing a long blonde wig and black rimmed glasses that swooped up on the sides stood behind a large glass case filled with a variety of wigs in outrageous colors; blue, yellow, green, orange, and rainbow. The beauty queen was busy reading People magazine. Her black framed rhinestone dotted glasses bobbed up and down on her nose as she chewed her gum which she occasionally blew into a bubble. The young lady's bright green blouse, short black skirt, fishnet stockings torn at the knees, and high black boots reminded Addison of a clown she'd once seen in a circus. Lady Large Boobs looked up and blew a large pink bubble as Addison came in the door. Neither of them spoke. The clown lady's eyes returned to the magazine. Her feet stayed glued to the floor as her jaws continued to give the bubble gum a strenuous workout.

Both side walls of the long narrow shop held shelves from floor to ceiling stocked with every wig and hair extension imaginable. The back of the shop held four small desks pushed up against an old brick wall. Large oval mirrors hung above each desk The shop was quiet except for the sound of Addison's footsteps on the squeaky wooden floor and the intermittent popping of bubble gum. Addison walked the full length of the shop carefully studying and picking out a variety of wigs and hair extensions that would provide her with several different looks.

She walked to the front of the shop and put them all down on the glass case. The young clerk sighed, set her magazine down, popped another large bubble and began ringing up the items without saying a word, never once looking up at Addison. When she was done ringing up all the items she tilted her head a little to the side, smacked the gum and said, "That'll be one hundred sixty-four dollars."

"She speaks," Addison said.

"What?"

"Nothing," Addison replied, as she handed the clerk the correct amount of cash, gathered up the hair pieces and headed for the door. She heard one last bubble pop as the bell jingled and the door closed behind her.

The Mercedes dealership which serves as the headquarters for Burton T. Caldwell's luxury auto empire is located on a hilltop in Aurora, Colorado overlooking Cherry Creek State park on the Southwestern edge of the city. The building is an ultra-modern two story glass and steel structure with a curved covered walkway over the first floor of the main entry. A giant Mercedes-Benz sign matching the curve of the building stands above the walkway and extends well past the top of the second story. The centerpiece showroom of the dealership holds eight different models of the famous automobiles. A sleek red SLS Class Coupe holds court on one side of the showroom at a starting price of two hundred-twenty thousand dollars. The opposite side of the showroom shows off a silver S65 AMG sedan. The balance of the luxurious showroom stable was made up of a variety of coupes and sedans ranging from $50,000 to $150,000.

Addison walked into the dealership wearing a black wig and oversized black-rimmed sunglasses which she kept on. She had chosen gray pantyhose to wear under a short black skirt and a gray blouse covered by a cheap short length fur coat she had picked up at Goodwill. She casually walked around the showroom running the tips of her fingers along the sides of one of the sporty coupes. She took a couple of steps back and pressed a finger to her lips as if she were trying to make up her mind.

A tall salesman wearing a blue pinstripe suit came over and introduced himself. "Hi, I'm Alan Bishop," he said. "Are there any questions you might have that I can answer for you?"

"Hmm, not really," she replied. "My husband ran off with his secretary and I got a big pile of money in the divorce. I'm just looking at ways to spend it. I don't know a thing about cars but these all seem pretty nice."

"It's hard to find an automobile that surpasses the quality and elegance of a Mercedes," Bishop replied.

"A friend of mine told me that if I wanted a great car then Burton Caldwell was the guy to go and see. Is he around?"

"Oh, he's around all right. He's always here, first one in early every morning and the last one to leave, usually long after everyone else has gone home; although he doesn't usually come down to the showroom floor. That's him in the corner office upstairs, the one with all the glass around it."

"Oh my, you mean the guy with the gun?" she said, as she looked up at the second floor, memorizing every detail.

"Yup, that's him. He's never without it. Folks here joke that he probably wears it in the shower."

Addison looked at her watch and said, "Oh, goodness, I didn't realize it was that late. I have an appointment with my divorce attorney in a half hour. I just have time to make it. Thanks very much Mr. Bishop. I'll come around next week and we can talk more seriously about which car I would look the best in." She took another quick look around the showroom and at Caldwell's office as she hurried out the door.

Addison drove to the Aurora library on East Hamden Circle not far from Cherry Creek State Park. She went to one of the computers, looked up the article on the recent recall election and printed it. She put on a pair of gloves, removed the article from the printer, carefully folded it and put it in her purse. She took a Handi-wipe out of the purse and carefully wiped all the keys on the keyboard, and the arms of the chair she'd been sitting in.

Chapter 12

Burton Caldwell grew up an only child in a very wealthy family. He was raised to believe he was better than most people. It was a trait that fit him like a glove. He never had any children of his own. He was on his third marriage and had a mistress he saw two nights a week. The mistress lived in a luxury apartment paid for by one of the dealerships. A large chunk of his fortune was spent paying alimony to wives one and two.

Caldwell's auto dealerships catered to wealthy people with beliefs similar to his own. He paid his salespeople well and his support people poorly. His political views made Tea Party conservatives look like candy-assed liberals. And of course his lifelong crusade was to protect and preserve the Second Amendment of the Constitution, the right to keep and bear arms. He wasn't a hunter but he was an excellent marksman. His mansion contained three gun safes, each stuffed with the newest, coolest weapons on the market. He had nearly every caliber of weapon available that was legal to purchase and one or two that weren't. There were handguns, rifles, shotguns, automatics, semi-automatics, six shooter revolvers and a variety of expensive antique weapons. Yes sir, Burton Caldwell believed every man, woman and child over the age of twelve was entitled to have, hold and shoot a gun of some kind.

Addison sat in her car across the street from the auto dealership watching the employees leave and lock up for the night. Just as the smooth talking Bishop had said; Caldwell was still at his desk long after everyone had left for the night. Addison was dressed all in black from head to toe. It was just past nine-thirty when she turned off the dome light in the Lexus and stepped out into the frigid night air, quietly closing the car door behind her. She stayed in the shadows as she made her way through the parking lot to a side door next to the service department. She put on a pair of latex gloves, used her lock pick set to open the door and slowly made her way down a long hallway to the showroom floor. The only light on upstairs was a lamp on Caldwell's desk. He was sitting with his back to the door; his feet propped up on the corner of his huge desk as he smoked a cigar and talked on the phone. He was wearing a nine-hundred dollar pair of ostrich skin cowboy boots, jeans and a white dress shirt. Smoke from his cigar drifted lazily into the air above his head.

Addison slowly climbed the stairs like a panther stalking its prey. She never took her eyes off Caldwell as she made her way to the top of the landing. She held the gun she'd taken from the drug dealer at her side, finger on the trigger guard. She took three quick, quiet steps and was standing directly behind the famous car pitchman. She slowly raised the gun and put her finger on the trigger.

"Sounds great, Jack," Caldwell was saying. "Give me a call next week and we'll meet at the club for lunch. We can talk about fundraising to get the rest of those liberal bastards out of office." As the conversation ended and Caldwell hung up the phone, Addison pressed the barrel of the drug dealer's gun against the back of Caldwell's head. He dropped the phone and froze. The expensive cigar clenched tightly between his teeth.

"I just wanted you to know," she said, "it took me all of two minutes to get this gun. It's one of thousands that are out there on the streets because of the lack of gun controls in this country thanks to people like you. This one came to me compliments of a drug dealer in Chicago." She pulled the trigger. The car dealer's head snapped forward, spitting out the cigar as the bullet passed through his brain and out his forehead. He died instantly. Addison took the article on the recall election out of her pocket and laid it in the center of Caldwell's desk. She laid the drug dealer's gun on top of the article and made her way back downstairs. She locked the door she had come through next to the service department as she left the building and hurried back to her car.

Becky Sanford screamed and dropped the tray she was carrying when she saw Caldwell's body. She was one of Caldwell's oldest employees in both age and tenure. She arrived a little after seven each morning; her routine was to make the coffee and carry a carafe, along with cream and sugar upstairs to Caldwell on an ornate silver tray. She took a step toward the body, gasped and put her hand up to her mouth. She had a sudden thought, "Was the killer still in the building?"

She ran back downstairs to her office, grabbed her purse and ran out of the building before dialing 911 on her cell phone.

Eight minutes after she made the call, two patrol units rolled up. Jim Pierson, a regular patrol officer and Wes Blackburn, a K-9 unit officer. Blackburn opened the back door of his patrol car and a huge German Shepherd jumped to the ground, eager to go to work. The officer led the eager canine to the employee entrance. He removed the leash, took his Sig Sauer 45 out of his holster, gave the dog a search command and followed him into the building. Pierson followed, Sig 45 in hand. The building was quickly cleared and the three of them returned to the parking lot. The exuberant Shepherd was put back in the K-9 unit. Both officers then secured the entire perimeter of the building with yellow police tape.

Detective John Fife arrived just as the two officers were finishing up with the yellow tape. Fife stepped out of his car holding a cardboard tray with three cups of coffee which he held out to Pierson and Blackburn as they approached.

"Thanks Barney," Pierson said as he took his cup out of the holder.

"Yeah Barney, thanks a lot," echoed Blackburn as he reached for the second cup.

Fife took the last cup and tossed the cardboard holder back onto the seat of his car where it joined several other empty cups and food wrappers.

Getting the moniker "Barney" was something Fife fully expected when he went into law enforcement. Bernard P. "Barney" Fife had been a bumbling police officer played by Don Knotts in the TV series Mayberry RFD. Although the show went off the air in 1971, you could still catch reruns on some of the stations that played the old shows. John Fife had become "Barney" the very first day he set foot in the police academy nearly twenty years ago.

"So, what've we got?" Fife asked as he pulled the lid off his cup of coffee. Blackburn took a sip from his cup and nodded at Pierson.

"We've got a body upstairs in what looks like the top dog's office. No sign of forced entry. Miss…." Pierson sat his coffee on the hood of Fife's car, took a small notebook out of his breast pocket, and flipped through the pages. "Miss Sanford, that's her over there," Pierson gestured with the notebook as he retrieved his coffee. "Miss Sanford says she arrived a little after seven and began her daily routine. She took coffee up to the boss like she does every morning and found him dead on the floor. No sign of a struggle, can't tell if anything is missing. Sanford says the outside door was locked when she got here just like it always is this time of day."

"Ok, Blackburn you and the hound go ahead and take off. Pierson, stand by while I have a chat with Miss Sanford."

Fife ambled over to Becky Sanford and introduced himself. She was leaning against her car with both arms crossed over her chest as if she were hugging herself to keep warm. The sun was shining and there wasn't a cloud in the sky but the temperature was in the mid-thirties.

"So, must've been quite a shock to you coming in and finding your boss like that," Fife said as he leaned against the car next to her.

"Yes it was," she replied. "Mr. Caldwell wasn't liked by a lot of people but he was always very nice to me. I've been working for him for nearly fifteen years."

"So can you think of any of those people who didn't like him that may have hated him enough to want him dead?"

"No, not really. I mean there were a lot of people upset about his involvement with this recall business but I don't see any of them wanting to kill him."

"Ok I'll tell you what, since you know all the regular employees, would you mind staying here a while longer and sending them home as they show up?" Fife took a drink of his coffee which was rapidly cooling in the frigid air. "We've got an active crime

89

scene here so nobody is going to be selling any cars today. As soon as you have sent all the employees home you can go. We'll get in touch with you a little later to get the names of all the folks who work here."

"Certainly," she said. "Anything I can do to help."

Fife walked back over to where Pierson was standing, took the last gulp of his coffee and tossed the empty cup into the back seat of his car. "Ok Jim, grab a roll of the red crime tape for the hot zone and let's go inside for a look see."

The scene was exactly as the two officers had described it. One dead guy on the floor, gunshot wound to the back of the head. No sign of a struggle and nothing seemed to be missing. The Medical Examiner showed up at the same time the Crime Scene Investigators arrived. The ME looked at the body, rolled it over and removed the victim's wallet. The ID confirmed it was Burton Caldwell. The wallet contained just over five hundred dollars in cash. The CSI's bagged the gun on the desk and the article under it, then began the tedious task of gathering prints and looking for other evidence. Fife headed back to his office to start gathering names for interviews.

Chapter 13

Addison drove to a small hotel in Louisville just northeast of Denver and a little off I-25. She purchased a copy of the Denver Post from a vending machine just outside the hotel lobby, checked in and went up to her room. She kicked off her shoes, turned on the TV and lay back on the lumpy bed. She flipped through the channels looking for any news about her recent activities. As she suspected, nothing was there, too early. The body probably wouldn't be discovered until morning. She was confident that nothing had been left behind that could tie her to the crime.

She scanned the headlines on the front page of the paper before turning to the classifieds. She was formulating her next move and needed another easy-to-get weapon. Nothing listed under guns or weapons anywhere in the classified section. She focused next on estate sales. There were several and each one had a partial list of items for sale. Addison scanned each one and found what she was looking for. The ad read, "Estate sale 9 a.m. to 5 p.m. Sunday. Jewelry, antique furniture, guns and other misc items for sale."

She arrived at 8:45 the next morning. The sale was in an old house in an upscale Denver neighborhood. There were several other early birds meandering through the old two story home looking at the various items. The place was packed with antiques in every nook and cranny. Who ever had died had good taste and knew what they were doing when they had furnished the place. Addison wore a long blonde wig, tight jeans, a yellow sweater and fashionable black high top boots. She was greeted by an elegantly dressed, slightly overweight woman with gray hair that was just a bit short of turning white. The woman was wearing tan slacks and a blue turtle neck wool sweater. She had a narrow pair of reading glasses perched on the end of her delicate nose and was looking at what appeared to be an inventory of the home's contents.

The woman looked up over the top of her glasses as Addison walked into the room.

"Hello, I'm Grace Weatherford," she said as she held out her hand. "Are you here for the estate sale?"

"Yes I am, my husband is a real gun nut and I saw that you had some listed for sale in your ad," Addison replied as she shook the woman's hand.

"Yes we do, two of them in fact. I really don't know a thing about them other than what the appraiser told me they were worth. They were my father's. He passed away four years ago. My mother passed away three months ago and we're finally getting around to dealing with the estate." The woman adjusted her reading glasses and looked at the inventory sheet. "Yes, here they are," she said. "There is a Ruger LCR .38 SPL, whatever that means, and a Sig Sauer Mosquito. Mosquito? What an odd name for a gun." The woman squinted and held the list closer to her face. Yep Mosquito, that's what it says.

The Ruger is four hundred and the Sig Sauer is three hundred. The appraiser said both were worth much more but at that price they would go quickly and that's what we want." The woman led Addison upstairs to the master bedroom walk-in closet where she retrieved the two gun cases from a shelf and laid them on the neatly made bed. She opened both cases for Addison to look at. "I am really afraid of guns and want to get them out of here as quickly as I can," she said.

"Well to tell you the truth I am a little afraid of them too," Addison lied. "I really don't understand what my husband sees in them, but I think I'll take them both. I'll give him one for his birthday and the other for Christmas."

"Oh, that would be wonderful," Weatherford said. "I just need to get your name and address for the records.

"Certainly," Addison replied. "The name is Wanda, Wanda Grisham. My address is 2700 Black Canyon Way in Castle Rock. Do you know where that is?"

"Yes, I do, just a little south of Denver," the woman replied as she jotted down the name and address.

Addison paid the woman with seven 100 dollar bills, thanked her for her time and left.

She returned to the hotel and laid both gun cases on the bed. She looked in the mirror, removed the blonde wig and brushed her hair back. The wig fit a little too tight and she felt like her head was about to explode. She massaged her head with the tips of her fingers.

She went to the bed and removed the Sig from its case. It was a very clean weapon with a four inch barrel adjustable sights and a polymer composite grip. She popped the ten round magazine out of the weapon, it was full. She pulled the slide open and a shiny twenty-two millimeter cartridge jumped out onto the bed. *Hmmm, I wonder if the old lady knew she had a loaded gun in the house, seven in the hopper and one in the chamber.* Addison took a closer look at the Ruger, it had a stainless steel cylinder that held five shots. It wasn't loaded, but there were a dozen cartridges laying loose in the case. Just like the Sig, the gun was in mint condition.

A pang of hunger stirred in Addison's stomach. She packed the guns away, picked up the newspaper and drove three miles south to an International House of Pancakes she had seen near the interstate. She ordered coffee and blueberry pancakes with a side of bacon. She sipped her coffee and casually scanned the newspaper while she waited for her breakfast. Two articles on page three caught her eye.

The first was about a Supreme Court case that had just been decided by a 5-4 decision with Justice Barker casting the deciding vote. Harold T. Barker was by far the most conservative of the nine. Appointed by the second President Bush shortly after he took office in 2001, Barker could always be counted on to provide the conservative vote on any issue from gun control to the environment. The most recent case involved a wealthy democrat, George Franklin, who owned several thousand acres of land in Montana but not the mineral rights. Somehow long before Franklin acquired the land, the mineral rights had been signed over to the Bureau of Land Management. Much to the dismay of Franklin the government decided to drill for oil on the pristine property. The plan was to develop fifty drilling sites. Franklin of course sued and appealed his way through the judicial system all the way to the Supreme Court. After five long and expensive years he had lost the case thanks to the deciding vote cast by Justice Harold T. Barker. The article also mentioned a couple of other cases in the judge's career where he decided in favor of the NRA when they were battling groups wanting stricter gun control laws.

The second article was about the NRA and the huge lobby arm of the organization. There are 34 lobbyists working for the NRA. Eighteen of the 34 are former government employees with critical access to senators and congressmen. The organization constantly reviews any legislation at state and federal levels that place any restrictions on gun ownership, background checks, etc. With a lobby budget of over three million dollars they work hard at influencing elections and decisions on gun control. Their deep pockets have influenced votes on issues from gun control to civil rights at nearly every level of government.

Addison's breakfast arrived. She put the newspaper aside and took a sip of her coffee. The wheels began to turn in her head. No wonder there is a lack of suitable gun controls in this country. The NRA lobby is clearly in control of Congress when it comes to issues of gun control. She took a bite of her blueberry pancake and decided she needed to do some research on the NRA lobbyists. What better way to send a message than to eliminate one or two lobbyists. She finished her breakfast and headed back to her hotel to do some research.

She logged on to the hotel's WiFi system, brought up Google and began searching for NRA lobbyists and events. Her search turned up a regional conference starting the first week in March in Eugene, Oregon. The event theme was "NRA, Making Your World A Safer Place." It was a three day affair for NRA members from Oregon, Washington and Idaho. The event included gun displays, speakers, seminars and tours of the local area. Sponsors included Cabela's, Glock, Beretta and various other producers of guns and ammunition along with the miscellaneous paraphernalia used in cleaning weapons, reloading bullets and so on. Several of the seminars were being presented by Gregory J. Townsend, the NRA lobbyist responsible for the Pacific Northwest region. Addison did more online research and found that Townsend had been a congressional aide for a republican congressman from

Louisiana. He'd gone to work as a junior lobbyist for the Institute for Legislative Action in 2002 when the congressman lost his seat to a liberal democrat. The Institute for Legislative Action, known as the ILA is the lobby arm for the NRA. Townsend had done well in his role as junior lobbyist. He was quick to spend money wining and dining state legislatures and clearly got results when it came to passing favorable legislation on gun controls.

Addison closed Google and brought up a map application on her laptop. She calculated a route from Aurora to Eugene. She used one of her alias's credit cards to do an online registration for the conference and to make a reservation at the Eugene Hilton. She figured the 1345 mile trip would be a fairly easy two day drive.

Chapter 14

John Fife just finished up four long days of getting nowhere. He'd gone over all of the previous month's credit card charges and phone calls made by the late Burton Caldwell, Mercedes Benz King of Colorado. He had found absolutely nothing zero, zip, nada that pointed in the direction of someone who would want Caldwell removed from the land of the living. He'd also questioned everyone at the car dealership from the lot boys to the mechanics to the sales staff. Other than the occasional reference to his political stance and possible enemies associated with it, not one single person could provide even the slightest clue or point him in a productive direction.

Fife was about to start calling people listed in Caldwell's Outlook contact list to see what he could dig up when his phone rang.

"Barney, it's Johnson down in the crime lab."

"Yeah Phil, what's up?" Phil Johnson was one of Fife's favorite crime lab techs. He'd been scouring evidence for over twenty years and never missed a thing. He knew more about guns and ballistics than anybody in the universe. Anytime a DA was working a case they wanted Johnson in the witness box. Those lucky enough to get him rarely lost.

"Well, we pulled the nine mil slug out of the wall in Caldwell's office, ran it through the NCIC system and got a hit. The slug matches one pulled out of some gang banger's body in Chicago last year. The gang guy may have been killed with the same gun that killed Caldwell. They found his body in Lake Michigan about three months ago. Their slug was in pristine condition, the body not so much. Anyway the slug appears to be a match to the one from our guy Caldwell, or at least Caldwell's wall."

"Great work," Fife said as he took a sip of very cold coffee from the Styrofoam cup on his desk. He gagged, made a face like he'd drunk sour milk and spit the coffee into the metal trash can next to his desk.

"What was that?" Johnson asked. "Sounded like a cat coughing up a hairball."

"Nothing, just took a drink of cold coffee. Geez, I hate it when I do that. The coffee here is pretty bad to begin with and drinking it cold could choke a horse." He dropped what was left of the cold drink into the trash can. The cold liquid in the cup splashed straight up at Fife as if it were trying to get in the last word. "Okay Phil, thanks a lot. I think I'll call the FBI folks in Denver to see if they want to get involved."

"Happy to be of service my friend. The next time I'm up your way I'll buy you a cup of real coffee."

Fife hung up the phone, opened the bottom drawer of his desk, leaned back in his creaky chair and put his feet up on the open drawer. He clasped his hands behind his head, looked up at the ceiling and took a deep breath. *"Hmm, might have finally caught a break."* *he said to the empty room.* He closed his eyes as he thought about why someone who killed a gang banger in Chicago would want to come to Colorado and kill a car dealer. It made no sense. It was more likely that the person who killed the gang banger didn't come to Colorado, but someone with the gun that killed the banger had come to Colorado, but why? And why did that someone go to the trouble to leave a copy of the article about the recall election on Caldwell's desk along with the murder weapon?

Fife sat up, pushed the desk drawer in and called the regional FBI office in Denver. He asked for the senior agent in charge and a familiar voice came on the line. "Barney, my fine detective friend, what have you gotten yourself into now? Is it the IRS coming after you for back taxes? Not sure we can help with that, or did you get busted for pirating movies. That warning at the beginning of the video is very serious you know. We could put you away for life on that one." It was Erick Jacobson. Fife and Jacobson were longtime friends. They met when Fife was a rookie cop and Erick was a newbie with the FBI. They'd worked a couple of bank robbery cases together and soon realized they shared a passion for fly fishing. Every couple of years they would get away from it all and spend a week fly fishing on the Gunnison River in Colorado smoking cigars, drinking good whiskey and swapping fish stories.

"Very funny Jacobson, I can understand my own people giving me a raft of shit, but I would expect a little more respect from a bunch of worthless pencil pushing feebs."

"Ha! Okay Barney we'll call this one a draw. So what's up?"

"I assume you heard about the demise of Burton Caldwell the Mercedes dealership guy."

"Yup, when we're done fighting crime for the day here in my neck of the woods we spend the rest of our free time drinking good coffee and reading newspapers, unless there's a good soap opera on TV to watch."

Fife explained the slug found at Caldwell's being a match to one found on a dead guy in Chicago and the article about the recall election found on Caldwell's desk. "I just wondered if you guys might have an interest in working with us on this one."

"Yes we would. And I've got just the guy to put on it. His name is Shawn Trotter. He was a beat cop in Houston who wanted to do more. He scored off the charts on all his tests and made it through the Academy just under the wire for the age limit. He's been on the job all of one week and I was just looking for something for him to do."

"Sounds good, but does he fly fish?"

"I'm not sure, but if he doesn't I'll toss his ass out the door."

At eight o'clock the next morning Fife arrived at his office to find Shawn Trotter in the waiting area. Trotter looked like most FBI agents. His reddish blonde hair was cut Marine short. He had a fair clean shaven complexion and came in at about five-ten and one seventy-five. Fife watched him as they walked back to the detective cubicles. He saw that Trotter had a distinctive walk, not what you would call a swagger, rather a gait of confidence. Fife poured them each a cup of coffee and they spent a few minutes getting to know each other. The FBI agent made a face when he took his first sip of the coffee concoction. Trotter had gone to Bible College and spent time as a youth pastor before joining the police force in Houston. Despite passing the detective exam Trotter had been passed over due to understaffing at the street patrol level. When it happened the second time he began exploring the possibilities of joining the FBI. He was first or second in nearly every category at the FBI Academy and was now excited to be a part of the Denver team. Fife handed Trotter the thick file on the Caldwell murder. He pointed to a desk in the corner of the room and said "Here you go sport, come and see me when you've gone through it all."

An hour later Trotter knocked and stepped into Fife's office. "So, what do you think?" Fife asked as Trotter took a seat.

"Well, looks like someone has an issue with gun control legislation and the way it's headed. I certainly don't see any kind of connection with the gang banger murder in Chicago other than the possibility of the same weapon being used in both murders." Trotter took a stack of files off the chair next to Fife's desk and dropped them on top of a bookcase in the corner of the office. He sat down in the chair and told the detective everything he had dug up on the Chicago murder, confirming that there probably wasn't a connection there at all. "So, what's next?" Trotter asked.

"Why don't you go down to the Mercedes dealership and re-interview some of the people there, starting with Caldwell's Executive Assistant. You may be able to come up with something I missed."

"Sounds good, I'll check back with you tomorrow," Trotter responded as he stood and headed out the door.

Chapter 15

Greg Townsend was 44 years old and kept himself in near perfect physical condition. He was fashion model handsome with dark hair that he kept the gray out of with an over-the-counter hair coloring product. He had developed a slight vision problem like most men at that age, but was too vain to wear glasses. He opted for blue tinted contacts which added to his handsome playboy persona. He was an impeccable dresser and had a silver tongue when it came to persuading legislators to see things the NRA way. He could communicate with corporate CEO's as well as spit and whittle loggers who carried their guns into the woods along with their chainsaws. He was also known to be quite the lady killer. He often flirted with and bedded more than one beautiful woman when he was on the road touting the gospel according to the NRA.

He checked into the Chrystal Suite at the Inn at the Fifth in Eugene two days before the conference was set to open. The luxurious suite featured 2 fireplaces, a 15 foot square immersion shower and a separate whirlpool. The room was perfect for entertaining politicians during the day and beautiful women at night. The lavish accommodation was a short walk to the Hilton where the conference was being held. The NRA lothario always arrived a day or two early to spend time wining and dining various state politicos to make sure they were on board with the NRA agenda. It also gave him the opportunity to explore the city night life to see where the best selection of beautiful women was to be found. He had never been to Eugene, but since it was a college town there were sure to be a fair amount of uninhibited college coeds looking for a good time.

Townsend had dinner with R.J. Bodenhamer and his wife at a recently opened steak house near the Hilton. R.J, a republican state legislator from Burns, Oregon owns a 3000 acre cattle ranch and spent half the evening sucking up the free flowing booze and talking about the wolves recently released in Eastern Oregon. Bodenhamer wore blue jeans, expensive leather cowboy boots and a white western style dress shirt decorated with a bolo tie that boasted a huge turquoise centerpiece. More fitting for New Mexico than Oregon but then he wasn't really known for his fashion sense. Mrs. Bodenhamer was a quiet, demur sort of woman who definitely took a back seat to her husband's business and political interests. She wore a conservative black dress with a high neckline and a hem that reached well below her knees. The outfit was adorned by one simple yellow butterfly broach. R.J. left his 200 dollar dress Stetson with the snake skin hat band on the back seat of his bright red, one ton, four-wheel drive Dodge truck which was currently taking up two parking spaces in the Hilton parking structure.

The overbearing rancher brought up the subject of wolves as the trio waited for their appetizers to arrive. "Damn giant dogs are gonna end up killing off the best of my herd if these liberal democrat bastards don't get off their asses and take stock of what they're doing. Wolves eat other animals and that's a fact plain as the nose on your face," he said. Throughout the entire evening's conversation Mrs. Bodenhamer never spoke a word. She merely nodded affirmatively at each of her husband's vociferous talking points, most of which that ended in "Isn't that right dear?" After talking about the wolves, devouring a large filet mignon and drinking a half bottle of expensive Merlot, the politician assured Townsend he was on board with the NRA agenda. He was quick to point out however, that "Oregon is one of the most liberal states and easing up on their gun legislation is going to be an uphill battle." Nothing Townsend wasn't already familiar with, he didn't get this far without doing his homework when it came to swaying the opinions of others. "Not a problem Mr. Bodenhammer, long as I can count on your support I think we can make it happen," Townsend replied as he finished the last swallow of the expensive wine.

After spending two hours listening to political rhetoric and the evils of wolves, Townsend dropped the windbag rancher and his wife at the Hilton and headed to the University district looking for some action. He settled on a brew pub on the west side of campus where he could hear loud music crashing its way into the street through the open door. The temperature was in the mid-forties and a light rain was falling, but the coolness and precipitation did nothing to dampen the spirits of the party animals headed into the pub. Townsend noticed a giant bouncer checking ID's as a steady stream of young shapely college girls flowed into the building drawn to the music like iron to a magnet. The NRA rep with the gift of gab found a parking spot two blocks away. He pulled his light jacket up over his head to ward off the rain and jogged to the pub. It was 9:30. The night was still young and Greg Townsend was looking for a roll in the hay with an attractive, young, slightly intoxicated, coed.

Townsend walked to the head of the line, nodded at the bouncer, put a twenty in the guy's hand and walked into party central. He found a table with two attractive coeds, and sat down in the empty chair at their table. "May I join you?" he asked as he sat without waiting for an answer. "I'm Greg" he said as he slapped a fifty dollar bill down on the table. "Now, what do the two of you like to drink?"

Amber and Melanie were typical starving college students looking to have a good time after a week of studying and it was clear Greg was there to show them both a good time. They were roommates living in an off campus hovel with three other girls. After a few drinks, Melanie, the less attractive of the two, felt a little woozy and a friend drove her home. "So, why don't we go back to my place and have a quiet drink to finish off the night?" Townsend suggested shortly after Melanie left. "Sure, why not?" came the slightly intoxicated reply from the lovely Amber. The rain had let up as Greg and his date walked back to his car. A short drive later Greg opened the door for her at his suite on Fifth Street. "This is where you live?" Amber said as she kicked off her shoes.

"Only for the next few days," Townsend replied. "What would you like to drink?"

"Forget drinking let's do something more fun," Amber said as she took off her blouse, tossed it on the floor and headed for the bed, shedding the rest of her clothes along the way. Townsend took a second to admire the shapely figure of the young lady then undressed and joined her on the bed. Five minutes later the huge bed was swimming with tangled sheets, naked bodies and lots of moaning.

When Townsend woke at just after five the next morning, Amber had already left. He had no idea when she left or how she got home, nor did he care. His mission had been accomplished.

Chapter 16

Addison headed north on I-25 to Cheyenne, then east on I-80 through the desolate southern plains of Wyoming. She'd seen several antelope herds grazing their way through the vast plains as day turned to night. She pulled over and got out to stretch her legs and looked up at the moonless sky. Millions of stars stared down at her through the darkness. She watched a falling star plunge toward the horizon trying to escape the confines of the atmosphere. She held her breath and listened to the total silence of the Wyoming prairie before getting back into the car and driving on. Three hours later she drove into Utah where she spent the night at a Hampton Inn near Salt Lake City. An early start the next day pushed her north through Idaho and into Oregon where she took highway 20 west across the high desert plains of Eastern Oregon. More herds of antelope dotted the landscape as she made her way to Bend, where she took highway 126 north then west. She wound her way along the McKenzie River through a forest of giant Douglas Fir trees and into Eugene. The drive along the river was beautiful with the sunshine filtering through the magnificent trees and bouncing off the crystal clear water. The city was named after Eugene Skinner, one of the earliest settlers in the area. Incorporated in 1862, the town of nearly 160,000 is home to the University of Oregon, a few high tech companies and a variety of lumber mills. The ever present counter culture population influence can be seen at a Saturday market in the heart of downtown in the summer and a huge three day festival called the Oregon Country Fair held in July each year on private acreage west of the city.

Addison drove into downtown Eugene at a little past five o'clock that evening. She spent an hour getting to know the streets and alleyways. Traffic was fairly light at that hour and a light rain was falling. She drove past what appeared to be a federal building with a dozen or so tents pitched in the courtyard entrance. She saw what she presumed to be a shabbily dressed tent occupant standing near the corner holding a sign asking for a handout. *God Bless, anything helps*, the sign read. A dog on a leash snoozed at the foot of the panhandler. Both dog and panhandler seemed oblivious to the rain. Both also looked physically fit and well fed. Addison wondered what it was about the guy with the sign that made him feel society owed him a living and whether or not putting the word God on the sign increased cash flow. Her research about the city indicated an annual rainfall of nearly 50 inches, easy to believe as the light rain turned heavy as she drove through the outskirts of the downtown area. She was looking for various quick access routes that would carry her out of town in a hurry. She found several options. The heavily traveled Interstate 5 runs north to Canada and south to Mexico and had a few easy access points from downtown. Also available was Highway 126 west to the coast or east, back the way she came in.

The rain had let up a little when Addison pulled into an Italian place for dinner. The poorly paved parking lot looked like a battlefield that had been bombed by the enemy. It had rain filled potholes that looked like they could swallow a small car. She dodged the water filled caverns and made her way up the sidewalk to the entrance. The place smelled of pizza and wood smoke. A petite brunette hostess politely showed her to a table near the window. She ordered a glass of wine and a bowl of Italian bean soup. Her gaze alternated between the flames of the wood fired pizza oven and the drizzle outside. She sipped her Merlot and started thinking of ways to meet the NRA lobbyist she'd read about, the one she had come to Eugene to kill.

After dinner Addison spent another hour driving around Eugene further refining her knowledge of the area. She continued her exploration of alleyways and parking lots that could be useful in a quick exit out of town. It was just after 8:00 pm when she finally parked in the structure underneath the Hilton and went to the front desk to check in.

She was greeted by a young polite collegiate-looking woman with dark brown hair and thick black rimmed glasses. "Good evening, welcome to the Hilton," the perky clerk said as Addison approached the front desk. Addison was wearing a dishwater blonde wig and wire rimmed glasses. She tried to look as unobtrusive as possible and wanted to check in with as little fanfare as she could. She carried her single bag up to her room on the third floor, dropped it off then spent the next hour exploring as much of the hotel as she could. She located fire escape routes, stairways, shortcuts through meeting rooms, kitchen areas and janitor's closets not knowing which, if any she might need for a quick exit or hiding place.

That night, as Addison slept, it wasn't Morgan and Joey that haunted her dreams; it was her last mission with the Looking Glass unit nine years earlier that came to her like a runaway freight train barreling through a tunnel. It was the mission that killed three Marines and nearly took her life as well. In her sleep, she closed her eyes tighter trying to push the nightmare out of her mind. She was there. She could smell the desert air and taste the dust drifting in through the open window of the Humvee as the convoy drove through the 110 degree Afghan night. She had gone in with a Seal team squad made up of three fire teams. The mission had been simple and had initially gone well. They had extracted one of the wives of a resident warlord who was going to give them vital information on Taliban movements. Addison's job was to comfort the woman and gain her confidence as they made their way back to the base then to help with the interrogation. The mission commander felt that the presence of another woman would be comforting to the woman they'd be picking up.

Addison and her charge were in the second vehicle of the convoy. It was total happenstance that a Taliban Guerilla group had seen the convoy coming from over a mile away. The Guerilla's had set up an ambush where the road passed between two large rock formations. Addison looked over the shoulder of

112

her driver just as the RPG hit the lead Humvee. The vehicle exploded into a ball of flame. She saw a soldier run out of the middle of the inferno, his clothing on fire. He made it just a few feet before one of the Taliban fighters killed him with a burst of fire from a Kalashnikov assault rifle, compliments of the failed Russian encounter with the Taliban several years earlier. The second RPG came directly through the windshield of the Humvee Addison was in. The warlord's wife was killed instantly as was the Marine sitting next to her. The explosion blew Addison out the back of the vehicle and into the middle of the road where she lay bleeding and in shock. The Seals in the last two Humvees were able to get out and return fire killing the entire Taliban group. Addison couldn't hear anything as she tried to sit up. She could taste blood but didn't know whose it was or where it was coming from. She looked at her left side and saw what appeared to be a piece of metal sticking out of it. Then she blacked out. Two weeks later Addison awoke in a stateside military hospital. There was no record of her ever having been involved in the skirmish or leaving the United States.

Addison sat up in bed, her body shaking as she slowly came to realize where she was. She ran her fingers over the long scar on her left side where the surgeon had removed a piece of the Humvee that had penetrated her skin and stuck in between two ribs. She went to the sink and splashed cold water on her face and took a few seconds to stare at herself in the mirror. Then she went to the window, pulled the curtains open and stared out at the rain-slicked

Eugene street below. She finally returned to bed where she focused on the blinking light of the smoke detector in the ceiling for a half hour as she tried to sleep. Nothing seemed to be working in her favor. She finally gave up on sleep and got up. She made herself a cup of bad coffee in the cheap coffee maker that came with the room and sat in the chair next to the bed with her feet propped up on the ottoman. She sipped her bad coffee and began to plan her day. After two more cups of the horrid concoction she had enough caffeine in her system to get up and shower. She put on a pair of red panties that could easily be seen given the right angle beneath the very short denim skirt she planned on wearing. A red blouse, large hoop earrings and the brunette wig completed the outfit she had chosen to catch the eye of Greg Townsend. She took the .22 Sig Sauer out of her purse and checked the magazine before re-inserting it and jacking a round into the chamber. She put the weapon back in her purse, slipped on her shoes and headed downstairs to the conference.

Chapter 17

Addison chose a front row seat near the end of the row and sat at a table that had no modesty panel. A short while later one of the local NRA people came in and gave a lengthy introduction of Greg Townsend talking about his exemplary college career, his stellar time as an aide to the Senator from Louisiana, and about how he was personally responsible for some key NRA agenda legislation getting passed in a variety of states. He finished by reading aloud the second amendment to the U.S. Constitution. "A well regulated militia being necessary to the security of a free state, the right of the people to keep and bear arms shall not be infringed, blah, blah, blah.

Townsend took the stage. He didn't bother to shake hands with the guy who introduced him. He carefully set his coffee cup and his notes on the lectern then pensively bit his lower lip for emphasis as he slowly scanned the room with penetrating eyes. As he looked toward Addison, she turned slightly towards him and slowly uncrossed and re-crossed her legs. It was only for an instant, but she clearly saw him glance down at her thighs. "My friends…" he hesitated for a few seconds for effect before continuing. "There is a danger lurking in this city, there is a danger in this county, there is a danger in this state, and there is a danger in this great country of ours," he said as he carefully paused after naming each entity, surveyed the audience again and continued to speak. "Our military complex is busy waging war all over the world and no one is watching out for our safety here at home. Immigrants are pouring over our borders at an alarming rate, gangs are killing and robbing innocent people in our neighborhoods, drugs and violence are taking over our cities and our schools. And where is the government that is supposed to be protecting us in our hour of need? They are busy trying to take away our guns!" A spontaneous applause broke out in the room. Townsend soaked up the applause like a sponge as he looked over at Addison and caught a glimpse of her red underwear taunting him from the confines of her short denim skirt.

After Townsend's speech, the conference recessed for an hour so the patrons could browse vendor exhibits and have coffee. Addison was adding cream and sugar to coffee when Townsend sidled up to her. "I don't believe we've met, Greg Townsend," the smooth talking NRA rep said to her as he pulled an empty coffee cup from the stack on the table. "Alicia Sanders," Addison responded.

"So are you from around here?"

"Just moved here from Gun Barrel City, Texas. Bought a place with some acreage about ten miles north of here. Thought I might try raising sheep. Got tired of the cattle business and the constant Texas droughts."

"Well maybe I could buy you dinner tonight and hear more about how a pretty woman goes from cattle ranching to sheep growing, or ranching, or whatever it is you do with sheep."

"Why Mr. Townsend, you do come on strong don't you? Are you always this assertive with the ladies?" Townsend said nothing; he just stood there and smiled. "I'll meet you in the lobby at 7:00 this evening," Addison said as she walked away with her cup of coffee and headed toward the Cabela gun display in the vendor area. She could feel him staring at her as she slowly walked away. *Gotcha scumbag,* she thought to herself.

Townsend was thinking of all the things he wanted to do to her body as one of the exuberant conference attendees came up to him carrying one of those plastic bags everyone gets for all their swag from the vendors trying to entice them into their booths. The fellow was wearing green camouflage cargo pants held up by red suspenders on top of a desert camouflage flannel shirt. The swag bag was bursting at the seams with NRA bumper stickers, a plastic 9 mm water pistol that was supposed to look like a Beretta, three baseball caps with different gun manufacturing logos and a variety of other things the average conference attendee can't possibly live without.

"So, what's your weapon of choice?" the military-trained-killer wannabe asked. Townsend glanced over the guy's shoulder to see Addison turning the corner into the ladies room. A picture of the beautiful brunette lying naked in his bed flashed into his mind as he turned back to answer the gun groupie's question.

Addison went up to her room and changed into sweat pants, running shoes and a hooded sweatshirt. After spending several days behind a steering wheel, she needed to get some exercise and fresh air. The air smelled of fresh rain and the temperature was in the low fifties as she stepped through the front door of the Hilton. She walked towards an unpainted concrete building next to the Hilton and saw that it was a performing arts center. She overheard a couple talking about the architecture style of the building. One of them said an entertainer had once referred to it as the world's largest paperweight. *A good description* she thought as she turned away from the building. She jogged north on Willamette Street then west on Fifth to Washington where she ran past the county jail. It was a formidable looking building made of red brick and dotted with the typical narrow slits used to provide windows for the jail birds. The entire structure was surrounded by a high chainlink fence topped with razor wire. She turned north on Washington towards the Willamette River. She passed a skateboard park where several juveniles in baggy pants were doing a variety of complex moves. Out of the corner of her eye she saw two of the dare devil boarders crash head on into each other.

· "Whoa, dude, that was sketchy, you shoulda bailed," she heard one of them say as they stood, shook their bodies and picked up their boards. She ran on and was just getting into a comfortable rhythm when she had to stop at a railroad crossing for an Amtrak train. She jogged in place as the train cars flashed by like frames in a movie. The humid air soaked up the environment and became heavy with the sounds and odors of steel wheels on steel rails infused with diesel exhaust from the giant locomotive. Screeching brakes pierced the air as the train slowed to a near stop as it approached the Eugene station. Addison continued her run north on a trail that took her under a canopy of huge oak trees and into a large park. She came to a path that paralleled the river and jogged west. She felt her body begin to relax as she hit a pace close to an eight minute mile passing walkers bundled up in hats and scarves to ward off the frigid air. The smell of trains and traffic was replaced with the moist smell of the river and the surrounding foliage. She heard a wolf whistle and turned to see five homeless looking people sitting around a picnic table passing a quart size beer bottle around. Each member of the scruffy group took extra long swigs trying to drain the bottle before the next one in line pulled the bottle away, anti-freeze for the coming night. Six empty bottles sat on the wet grass next to the table.

A little over an hour later Addison was back in her room at the Hilton. She was a little tired but pleased that she was still in good enough shape to run a little over six miles. After a quick shower and a nap she began to focus on how her evening was going to play out. She went downstairs to the business center of the hotel, logged onto the internet and printed off statistics on the amount of money the NRA spends lobbying. After that she printed off several articles about school shootings and clipped all the information together, folded it in half and put it in her purse being careful not to leave any finger prints on any of the pages. She went back up to her room, put on a short, form-fitting black and white striped knit dress and flat shoes, checked the clip in the Sig in her purse and headed downstairs to meet Townsend. He was wearing blue jeans, tan loafers a white shirt and navy blue blazer.

Townsend held out his arm in a gentlemanly fashion and she took it as they walked the two short blocks across 6th street and over to the 5th Street Market. In addition to the exclusive Inn at the Fifth where Townsend was staying, the complex included a variety of upscale shops and an elegant restaurant known for its expensive meals and stylish atmosphere where the NRA womanizer had made dinner reservations. The cozy eatery smelled of fresh baked bread, steaks broiling on the grill and expensive wines. The floor was covered in thick plush dark brown carpet. The walls were painted in earth tones and each cozy booth featured a variety of artwork on the walls. Low level sconce lighting added to the ambience. They sat across from one another in the comfortable booth. Townsend had a Chivas on the rocks and Addison had a Vodka Martini. When the second round of drinks came he slipped off his shoes and gently began to rub the inside of her calf. She returned the favor. As they ate their dinner, his foot slowly moved up her thigh to the hem of her short skirt. What he was after was clear and she did nothing to dissuade him from his conquest.

After dinner they went up to his room. He had already lowered the lights and had soft music playing in the background. He held her in his arms and kissed her deeply as he gently kicked the door shut behind him. "Hold that thought," he said as he made a quick trip to the bathroom. While he was gone she took the Sig out of her purse and slipped it under the center pillow on the bed. She was taking a chance, but was sure he wouldn't notice given what he had on his mind. When he returned she excused herself and went into the bathroom where she slipped out of her knit dress.

She came out of the bathroom wearing only her black lace bra and panties. She glanced over expecting to see him waiting for her and saw the Sig laying in the middle of the bed. Then it happened. Townsend seemed to materialize out of nowhere. He had been standing next to the bathroom door waiting for her. Before she could react he slammed her head against the wall and kicked her feet out from under her. Putting the gun under the pillow hadn't been such a good idea after all. The side of her head throbbed and her vision was blurred from the impact. As she lay on her stomach struggling to regain her senses she felt his body drop down on the back of her legs.

" So, is this is the way you like it?" he asked, as he leaned down and licked the back of her ear. He grabbed her wrists and pulled her arms behind her before she could react. "Rough sex has always been my favorite, only without a gun." She struggled to get to her knees but couldn't move. He outweighed her by a good 40 pounds or more and had caught her completely off guard. With her arms pinned back she had no leverage to move. *Damn!* She thought to herself, *how could I have been so stupid?*

"So tell me, Alicia, or whatever your name is, what were you planning on doing with the gun? I thought we had a special connection. I was laying there waiting for you, adjusting the pillows when I found it." He pulled both her wrists higher up her back. It felt like her shoulders were going to pop out of their sockets. "Don't make me have to ask you again" he said, as he once again leaned close to her ear. That was the opening she needed. She arched her back and snapped her head back as hard as she could, catching him on the bridge of the nose with the back of her head.

"You bitch!" he yelled as he let go of her wrists and grabbed his face. With her wrists free she was able to turn over onto her back. She sat up and caught him in the chin with the palm of her hand. She could see the blood gushing out of his snout as he struggled to stand. He left a trail of blood as he took one step and leaped onto the bed grabbing for the gun. She turned, stood and started for the bed hoping to beat him to the gun. The one step head start was all he needed. He turned and fired as she flew at him. She felt the sharp sting as the .22 caliber bullet passed through her left side just above her kidney. Her

122

momentum carried her on top of him before he could get off a second shot. As she landed she slammed her knee into his groin and grabbed for the gun. It easily came free as he writhed in agony from the painful kick. She pulled it out from between them shoved it against the side of his head and pulled the trigger. He jerked once and went limp as the life drained from his body. She rolled onto her back and stared at the ceiling. Her side was beginning to throb from the wound as blood dripped on the sheets of the king size bed. Two shots had been fired. With any luck it would have sounded like two bottles of champagne being opened and no one would be the wiser but there was no time to waste. She had to get out of there. She felt a slight sense of panic at the thought of the blood from her wound on the bed sheet. She wondered if it could somehow be traced back to her.

Addison rose from the bed and ran to the bathroom. She grabbed a large bath towel wrapped it around her middle and tied it to stem the flow of blood before pulling on her dress. She grabbed a smaller towel and thoroughly wiped down the gun and every surface she had touched. She pulled the papers she had printed at the Hilton from her purse, laid them on the bedside table and placed the gun on top of them. She had also typed a quick note at the Hilton that she added to the pile - *.22 caliber Sig Sauer purchased at an estate sale – no background check. Guns are easy to get.* She was about to leave when there was a slight knock and the door of the room began to open. It was room service delivering a bottle of champagne that was supposed to have been there an hour earlier. Addison quickly returned to the bathroom and pulled the door shut. She heard a scream as the person delivering the champagne saw the body and the blood. She held her breath and listened carefully for the footsteps of the person leaving. A smarter staff member would have picked up the phone and dialed 911, but this one simply screamed and ran out looking for a supervisor.

Addison took one last quick look around and stepped into the hallway through the open door. She could hear sirens in the background. Someone had already called 911. She looked to her right and saw a hotel maid and a male supervisor coming her way. The man's voice called to her as she quickly turned the opposite direction and stepped through the door marked stairs. She was glad she'd worn flat shoes as she took the steps two at a time racing to the ground level. She listened for footsteps as she made her way down and was relieved to see that no one had come after her. She walked to the intersection, crossed Sixth Street and made her way back to the Hilton where she sprinted up the stairs and into her room pressing her hand to her side as she went. She took off the dress and towel to look at the wound. The bleeding had slowed but not stopped. The entrance wound was almost perfectly round and about a quarter inch in diameter. She slipped her left hand down her lower back until she felt the exit hole and probed it with her finger and was relieved to find that it had been a through and through. If there had been damage to any organs she would have felt much worse. The biggest risk now was keeping it clean and free of infection. She wrapped the bloody towel back around her slim waist.

She took off the brunette wig and replaced it with a blonde one, changed into sweats and running shoes, wiped down every surface in her room, gathered her belongings and made her way out the front door of the Hilton. As she was walking out she passed a gentleman who was on his way in. Their eyes met for a brief instant. *Jack Wilder, what the hell are you doing here?* She quickly looked down and hurried on her way. Addison knew Jack from their early days together in the CIA Looking Glass program. They had gone through several training sessions together. She had a strong romantic interest in him at the time but never acted on it. She knew that no good could come from it. She wondered if he'd recognized her and hoped he hadn't.

She pulled out of the parking garage and turned left on Seventh then left onto Coburg road where she followed the signs that led to highway 126 and East towards Bend being careful to obey the speed limit not wanting to draw any unnecessary attention to herself. She made the quick decision to leave the same way she'd come into town. She needed to get as far away from Eugene as quickly as she could.

The moon was full, its bright beams bouncing off the rapidly flowing McKenzie River as the great waterway followed its well worn path westward to join up with the Willamette River. Addison lowered the window allowing the cold air in. She needed something to keep her awake and focused as she painfully drove through the night towards her destiny, wondering how it all would end. Getting shot by the sexist NRA lobbyist certainly hadn't been a part of her plan. She thought back to everything that happened in his room. Did she manage to sanitize the place well enough to keep the authorities off her trail? Was her message getting across?

Addison glanced out the window at the beauty of the river. When she looked back at the road a deer stood in the middle of the highway frozen in her headlights. She slammed on the brakes and turned the wheel to the left barely missing the creature, took a deep breath and winced at the pain in her side as she got the car back on a straight path.

Addison drove until she was exhausted. The pain in her side gave her a jolt with every bump in the highway. She pulled into a rest area somewhere in Utah off Interstate 80 where walked around the parking lot taking deep breaths trying to clear her head. The pain from the bullet wound had lessened, but only slightly. She climbed back behind the wheel, laid the seat back and slept for two hours. In her sleep she found herself back in the convoy in Afghanistan, only this time it was Joey and Morgan sitting with her in the back seat of the Humvee. The RPG came through the windshield killing them as Addison felt herself being pulled out of the vehicle by some unseen force. She could hear herself screaming for her loved ones as the force pulled her further and further away from them.

She was startled awake by an eighteen wheeler that pulled into the rest area. She watched as the driver climbed down out of the big rig and headed for the men's room. As soon as he went inside, Addison got out and opened the passenger door of his truck. She looked around and found a first aid kit under the seat which she quickly grabbed. She headed for the ladies room, went into a stall and took off her shirt to examine the wound. It was a little red and puffy, but showed no signs of infection. She took an alcohol swab from the kit and cleaned the wound, gritting her teeth to keep from crying out, then covered the wound with gauze and taped it as best she could. She stuffed the bloody towel from the hotel into the trash can before heading back to her car.

She walked back out into the cold night and looked up at the moonlit sky. Thousands of stars stared down at her like so many eyes watching her every move. Another eighteen wheeler drove in as she got into the old Lexus and pulled back onto the interstate. She didn't know why, but she was compelled to head East. She mulled over what her next step should be as she drove; another NRA lobbyist, maybe NRA headquarters, or maybe something or someone even bigger? She had several hundred miles ahead of her to figure it out.

Chapter 18

Sergeant Victoria Miller was at home. She'd just finished tucking her eight-year old son into bed and was turning out the light when her cell phone vibrated. "Sergeant Miller, this is Carol in dispatch. We just got a call from Officer Swanson who responded to a 911 call at the Inn at the Fifth. He said it appears to be a homicide. He's taping off the area now."

"Damn it," Miller responded. I was hoping for a quiet evening at home. Ok, call the Medical Examiner. I'll call a couple of my people and head down there as soon as I can."

Victoria "Vik" Miller was a 20-year veteran of the Eugene Police Department and had been head of the Violent Crimes Unit for just over two years. She had done 18 years on the streets before passing the Sergeant's exam and moving into Violent Crimes. She was always able to hold her own amongst her male peers on the street and had quickly gained the respect of the detectives in her unit. She was an attractive woman who stood just over five-five and maintained her trim figure with strenuous daily workouts and yoga. She kept a yoga mat in the corner of her small, neatly organized office. The thing she hated most about the job was that it was 24-7 every day of the year. There was never any time to decompress as she moved from one case to another and constantly dodged the political bullets that came with the job.

She headed downstairs and into the den where her husband was watching TV and drinking a Corona. "What's up babe?" he asked.

"Homicide downtown at the Fifth Street Market in the swanky new hotel."

"Well that sucks. That's the third one this year isn't it?"

"Yup. Sorry, but I've gotta head down there. Don't wait up."

She had a very understanding husband. A huge part of that understanding came from the fact that he was a police officer in nearby Springfield and knew exactly the kinds of issues she faced on a daily basis.

"I'll call Marilyn next door to come over and get Jonathan ready for school if you're not back when I leave," he said as she hurried out the door.

She called two of her best detectives, Brett Stevens and Ted Williams as she drove and assigned them to the case. Stevens was heavy set with grey hair, a bushy mustache and in his late fifties. The suits he wore somehow always looked like he had slept in them. What he lacked in clothes style he more than made up for in intelligence. He had a keen eye for looking at a crime scene and putting himself in the place of the killer. Williams was the polar opposite of Stevens when it came to fashion. He was an immaculate dresser any time of day or night. He was always wearing a clean white shirt, tasteful tie and slacks that looked like they had a permanent crease. He was slender, stood about five-eleven and had the build of a runner. He too, had a keen mind when it came to looking at crime scenes. The two of them together made a helluva team when it came to analyzing evidence and catching bad guys. On the way to the crime scene Stevens had also summoned Monica Summers, the newest detective in the unit. He knew there would be a need to knock on doors and Monica needed that experience. All three of them had already arrived at the scene when Vic drove up.

Brett Stevens met her in the parking lot as she pulled in.

"So, tell me what we've got," she said as she got out of the car.

"The victim is male, approximately 45 years of age. We'll know more as soon as the doc finishes up and lets us start working the scene. Front desk says the room is registered to a Greg Townsend. I called Monica in, she's out knocking on guestroom doors to see if anybody saw or heard anything useful.

Stevens took the steps two at a time as he led her up to the third floor room where the killing had taken place.

"So Frank, you're not gonna screw up my crime scene are you?" Vik said as she walked into the room. Frank Pratt was the Medical Examiner. He and his clothes had something in common. The suits he wore were from the late sixties and he was in his late sixties. He was more than a little overweight and nearly bald with only a few stray remnants of gray hair clinging desperately to his shiny dome. He wore thick wire rimmed glasses which were constantly sliding down his long narrow nose. His face was a ruddy pink from the pressure of moving his overweight body around. He was writing notes and looked up when he heard Vik's voice.

"Oh, it's you," he said with a grin as he stopped his note taking and turned towards her. "I was hoping they would send someone who knew what they were doing. I guess it's hard to get good help these days." Without missing a beat she smiled and replied, "Oh no, not you again. I was also hoping they would send someone who knew what they were doing, just this once."

"Ha," he said as he laughed and pushed his glasses up the bridge of his nose. "So how have you been Vik?"

"Ah you know, same old stuff. Fighting the frickin politicians and trying to catch the bad guys, all the time trying to keep ahead of which ones are which. So what are you thinking?"

"Gunshot to the head, looks like small caliber, probably 22, close range. Time of death about two hours ago, maybe a little more but not much. He probably died within a few seconds of being shot. I'll know a little more when I get him on the table."

He stood, looked around to make sure he hadn't left anything and pushed his glasses into place again. "Ok kiddo, it's all yours," he said. "Always glad to be of service, good luck and good night." He scooted past everyone, ducked under the tape and headed out the door.

Vik looked over at Stevens who was squatted down opposite the bed carefully studying something in the wall. He took a small knife out of his pocket and dug a slug out of the wall. "Hmm, this is interesting. Looks like a .22 slug and we have a .22 Sig sitting on the night stand. Someone put one in the wall and one into the guy's head." He closed his mouth and puffed his cheeks out. "Now that just doesn't make sense, no sir, none at all. If you have the gun, why shoot the wall and then the guy, or the guy then the wall? And, why leave the gun, especially when there's a river a few blocks away you can toss it into?" Stevens dropped the slug into a small plastic evidence bag. "And look at this" he continued, "a pretty good size pool of blood on the bed sheets. The guy somehow got his nose pounded in the scuffle, but that blood is quite a ways from the other puddle. Ten to one says that puddle of blood is from someone else."

Williams came walking out of the bathroom where he'd been looking for evidence. "Now, here's another thing of interest," he said, "There seems to be a towel missing from the bathroom. No sign of anyone taking a shower, but a towel is missing. I'm thinking find that towel and it will have blood on it that matches the puddle on the bed. Find the towel, find the shooter."

Vik pulled on a pair of latex gloves and lifted the Sig from the night stand, engaged the safety and dropped it into an evidence bag. She picked up the note that was under the gun. "Well, here's something weird," she said. "A note that says, This Sig Sauer was purchased at an estate sale – no background check. Guns are easy to get. Looks like somebody is trying to tell us something." She dropped the note into a separate evidence bag. "The serial number is still on the Sig, be sure and have the lab run it. If it was purchased at an estate sale maybe we can trace the owner and with a little luck, the buyer.

Monica Summers came into the room. "Anything useful?" Stevens asked.

"Zippo, boss. The room next door is unoccupied and the people two doors down heard a noise that they thought was champagne being opened. The night manager said he saw a woman at the end of the hall as he was coming to investigate. Said he called to her, but she was headed out the stair exit. He thought maybe she didn't hear him since she didn't stop or look in his direction."

"Get a description?"

"White female, brunette, slender, maybe mid-forties, wearing a short black and white dress."

"Be sure that gets in the book," Victoria said. "It may be important later. Could be a witness, could be the shooter or could be nothing. Check any business that was open in the area. See if anyone else remembers her. It would be great to find her and have a little chat."

Chapter 19

It was just past 7:30 in the evening when Jack's flight arrived in Eugene. He rented a car with GPS and punched in the address for the downtown Hilton. The temperature was in the low forties and the night was clear with a full moon. He parked in the circle drive of the Hilton and headed in to register. As he was going in, an attractive blonde woman dressed in sweats hurried through the door towards him. Their eyes met for a second before she quickly looked down and went on her way. Jack had a sense he somehow knew the woman, but couldn't quite place her. Someone from his past perhaps? Something in those eyes and the way she carried herself tugged at his memory banks. He was sure he had seen her before but couldn't figure out where. He racked his brain searching for the right memory, but came up blank as he turned and watched her hurry away.

Early the next morning Jack found himself standing on the sidewalk with a cup of coffee in his hand looking up at an old house on High Street near the University of Oregon. The house was the official home of the Citizens for Responsible Environment and Energy Protection, CREEPS. The place was probably built in the 30's with a high pitched roof and lap siding painted a light grey with dark blue trim. The front yard featured very little landscaping and a badly cracked sidewalk leading to the front door. A large, three foot by five foot sign displaying the CREEPS name and logo stood to one side of the sidewalk. The logo was a marijuana leaf surrounded by fir trees with what looked to be a stream of some kind flowing diagonally through the trees and under the marijuana leaf.

As Jack stepped inside he was greeted by a receptionist. A name plate on the counter that separated them said Sunshine. She was in her late forties and her long stringy hair was dyed in shades of orange, red and blue. She was wearing a large sweatshirt with a peace sign logo that covered the entire front and a long multi-colored cotton skirt and no shoes. Some of the colors in the skirt matched those in her hair.

"Hi, welcome to CREEPS. How may I help you?" she said as Jack approached the counter.

"I'd like to speak to the person in charge of your organization."

"Certainly, may I tell him what it is in regard to?"

"Actually, it's a private matter of a personal nature. I was sent here as a representative of the U.S. Supreme Court."

"Oh my," Sunshine responded. "Please wait here and I'll get Rick. He's the one in charge today. There are actually three co-managers of our organization and they each spend one week a month being in charge. The fourth week the office pretty much runs itself."

Jack stood at the counter and took a sip of his coffee as he surveyed the surroundings. He saw a few older desks, a photocopier and a wireless printer. The people he could see all looked to be hippie remnants of the sixties. The office equipment, on the other hand, seemed to be state of the art.

A short while later a tall lanky guy with a well trimmed beard and shoulder length grey hair came into the reception area. He held out his hand introduced himself as Rick Burke.

"How can I help you Mr….."

"Wilder, Jack Wilder. Is there someplace private we can talk?" Jack asked.

"Certainly, follow me," the gangly co-co manager replied.

Jack followed the CREEP executive down a narrow hallway and into a small office that appeared to be one of the home's small bedrooms. "So, how can I help you?" Rick said as he took a seat behind an old wooden desk and gestured toward a chair for Wilder. Jack leaned back in his seat and took a second to study Burke's face.

"Well, here's the thing Rick. I am here on behalf of Supreme Court Justice Harold Baker. He's been getting some threatening letters in the mail and we have reason to believe they may have come from this office." Jack took one of the letters out of his pocket and laid it on the desk for Burke to read. The CREEP leader leaned forward and read the letter without picking it up.

"Oh crap, he's really gone and done it now," Burke said as he leaned back in his chair. He picked up his phone and dialed the extension for the receptionist area.

"Sunshine, do you know where Shadow is?" Wilder thought to himself, *Sunshine, Shadow, these people are weird.* Burke frowned at Sunshine's response. "Well, make some calls and track him down. Tell him we need him here at the office, now." He placed the receiver back on the phone and looked up at Jack.

"One guy, one frickin guy is going to single handedly destroy everything this organization has worked for. His name is David Wells. He goes by Shadow. He has volunteered here for just under a year and is always outspoken about how we should use violence to get the attention of the politicians and lawyers to get our point across. He says that's the only way to get their attention. Believe me, that's not what we're about. I can't say for sure, but I think he's probably the one behind this. We caught him writing threatening letters a few months ago to a local judge who had ruled against us on an issue." Burke picked a pencil up and bounced it up and down on his desk to burn off some of his anger. "Fortunately we found the letters in the outgoing mail and they never got sent out. Everyone in the office knows that nothing is to

138

go out without the peace committee reviewing it first. We warned him about it. He apologized and said it wouldn't happen again."

Jack watched as Burke stood and began pacing back and forth in the small office. Halfway through his third lap a short skinny guy with long stringy hair and a scraggly beard came into the room. He looked to be about five-four and may have weighed one-thirty if his pockets were full of rocks. He was wearing blue jeans torn at the knees, an old Grateful Dead sweatshirt and no shoes. The scrawny guy went directly to one corner of the room and stood with his back to the wall without speaking a word.

"Jack Wilder, meet David Wells," Burke said as he stopped pacing and sat back down. "David, Mr. Wilder is here on behalf of the U.S. Supreme Court. It seems one of the judges has been receiving threatening letters that may have come from this office. Do you know anything about that?"

"My name is Shadow, don't call me David."

"Ok Shadow, do you know anything about the letters Mr. Wilder is referring to?" Wells looked up for a second. His eyes darted around the room like a caged animal looking to escape, then he quickly looked back down at the floor.

"Nope, don't know anything about it." Jack could tell from the guy's face and eyes that he was lying. He'd seen the same behavior in the countless number of people he'd interrogated during his tenure with the CIA. Wells quickly turned and left the room.

"As you can see Mr. Wilder, David is a little odd to say the least. We will change the locks and inform him that his days as a volunteer for our organization are over. Beyond that I don't know what else we can do."

"You've been a great help," Jack said. "The only other thing I need from you now is his home address and phone number for my report."

Burke turned to his computer, punched a few keys then scribbled the address on a post-it note and handed it to Wilder. "Here's his address, no phone number is listed." Jack thanked Burke for his time and headed back to his hotel where he had a quick lunch before heading out to find the home of David "Shadow" Wells.

Jack called Barry "Wonder Boy" Godley. He could hear a K. D. Lang song playing in the background as Barry answered. The guy was a heavy country music fan.

"Still a country music fan," Jack said. "When are you gonna learn to like real music?"

"Naw man, those beer drinkin boys with their pickup trucks and lonely heart girlfriends are what's happening. They know the true meaning of life although I think Paul Simon is kinda cool with some of his stuff."

"Oookay. So listen, I have another quick favor to ask."

"Ask away Jacko," Barry said as he took a slurp of his high octane energy drink.

"I think you were right on with your assessment of these Oregon CREEPS. I have zeroed in on a guy named David Wells"

"Of course I was right. Barry knows all, looking up David Wells as we speak. Ok, here we go. Mr. Wells was a trust fund baby. The only child of wealthy parents, raised by a nanny, attended private schools, graduated from Yale with a Physics degree. Both parents deceased, inherited around six million and dropped off the grid until he reappeared in Oregon about a year ago. No criminal records, not even a parking ticket."

"Ok, thanks kid, I owe you yet another one. Maybe I'll send you tickets to a country music festival sometime."

"Happy to be of service spy master, keep your head down, it's a jungle out there."

Wells' house was a small cottage sitting in the middle of several acres about 15 miles west of Eugene. A long dirt drive led from the highway to the slightly dilapidated home. What yard there may have been at one around the small place was totally overgrown by blackberries and other various weeds. There seemed to be no other vehicles anywhere on the property. Jack drove his rental around behind the house and parked it out of sight. He quietly climbed the steps of the back porch and found the back door unlocked. He let himself in and did a quick walkthrough to make sure the house was empty. There was a small kitchen just off the back porch, a small living room and one bedroom with a bathroom off the hallway that separated the kitchen from the bedroom. The living room had a wood stove that looked to be the only source of heat. The entire place couldn't have been more than 800 square feet. The center of the kitchen consisted of an old table of the Goodwill variety and two chairs that didn't match. The living room held a couch and a coffee table that also looked to be early Goodwill. Jack chuckled to himself as he realized both he and Mr. Wells shared similar tastes in furniture. He took one of the chairs from the kitchen and placed it in the center of the small living room. Then he settled into the old couch and waited. He had been sitting there a couple of hours when he heard the sound of a car coming up the drive. He glanced out the window to see an old VW bus chugging up the dirt drive. Jack stood next to the front door and waited.

Wells had barely stepped into the room when Jack grabbed him by the front of his shirt and slammed him against the wall while kicking the door shut. He then grabbed the surprised young man by the back of

142

his shirt collar, drug him to the middle of the living room, threw him into the waiting chair and gave him a quick slap across the face. The surprised Wells had no time to react or try to defend himself.

"What the hell, man!," Wells exclaimed as he started to stand. Jack didn't give him the chance. He gave him another slap and the guy collapsed back into the chair.

"Now listen to me, you little twerp," Jack said. "You know and I know that you're the one who sent those letters to Justice Baker. Are you still going to deny it?"

"I don't know what you're talking about Dude." Jack raised his hand again getting ready to give the scraggly little guy another slap. In the grand scheme of things this guy was nowhere near the bad guys Jack had dealt with in his past life as a CIA operative. The kid was a scared lightweight with no ability to fight back. "Ok, ok," Wells exclaimed. "Just quit slapping me. Yes, I sent the letters and I'm glad I did it. Baker is an idiot. He and half the government are responsible for ruining the environment and somebody needs to stop them."

"Ok, you scrawny little rat, I want you to listen to me closely because I'm only going to say this once. You are going to stop threatening Justice Baker and anyone else in the government. If you don't, I'm going find you wherever you may be and chop you into little pieces. Believe me when I say I will find you. I have the resources to do it. I've found and killed guys much higher up the food chain than you." Jack took a step back to study the look on Wells' welted face. Wells looked back at him for a few seconds then looked at the floor. Jack squatted down where his face was level with the scared Wells. He leaned in close to the young man, grabbed a handful of hair and tilted the guy's head back. Then he stared into the kid's eyes with a look that could kill and said, "Are we clear on this?"

"Yes we are. No more letters or threats, I promise." Jack stood and left the trembling Wells sitting in a urine soaked chair. As he opened the door Jack turned back to Wells and said, "I can find you anytime, anywhere." Jack left, confident he'd seen and heard the last of David "Shadow" Wells. On his way back to his car he noticed the little weasel's 1968 VW van in the driveway. The old relic sported the obligatory Grateful Dead sticker on the back bumper and contained stacks of fast food wrappers, empty soda containers and a couple of sleeping bags spread out across the back.

Wells changed clothes and went out to his van where he retrieved the bomb making supplies from beneath the sleeping bags. He carried the bomb paraphernalia into the kitchen table of the small cottage. It took two trips to gather everything. He was working on his third bomb; he had set the other two off on a remote logging road in the Cascade Mountains. It was all part of his plan to build the perfect, untraceable bomb. The third one would be used to dispose of Justice Baker. *We'll see who does what to who Mr. Government man Jack Wilder.*

Chapter 20

Fife was leaning back in his chair with his arms behind his head and his feet up on the desk when agent Trotter came in carrying two cups of coffee from Starbucks.

"Bless you my son," Fife said as he took one of the cups from Trotter. "I was just wishing for a good cup of coffee."

"Glad to be of service," Trotter responded. "And, I have something else you may have an interest in. I was perusing through the data bases this morning and found an interesting item. There was a homicide in Eugene, Oregon and the killer left a note behind saying the weapon came from an estate sale where there was no background check. Sound familiar?"

"Golly gee whiz, or to put in law enforcement terms, holy crap you might be onto something. Where'd you say it happened?"

"Oregon, Eugene, Oregon."

"That's fan-frickin-tastic!"

"How so?"

Fife took a sip of his coffee and cast a broad smile towards the FBI agent.

"It's so, because not only do we get to go to Eugene to investigate a homicide, we get to spend some time fly fishing on the McKenzie River. You do fly fish, don't you?" Fife sensed some hesitation as if Trotter was trying to decide what his answer should be.

"Well uh, actually I don't but I've always wanted to learn." Trotter responded as he drew in a long breath and hunched up his shoulders.

"Hmm," Fife looked down at the floor and shook his head. "Well, we'll work it out. You investigate and I'll fish, or we'll both investigate, then I'll fish. Oh hell, I can't do that. I'll just have to help you investigate and teach you how to fly fish. You're gonna love it. If you don't I'll just toss you into the river and that will be the end of it. The feebs back in Denver will never miss you."

United flight 832 touched down in Eugene at 9:00 A.M. the next day. A half hour later Fife and Trotter were in a rental on their way to police headquarters with Fife's fly fishing gear safely tucked away in the trunk. Trotter had phoned ahead and made arrangements to meet with Victoria Miller to discuss the case. He was thinking about the case similarities and the questions he wanted to ask Miller. Fife, of course, was thinking about which flies would work best on the McKenzie this time of year. Fife had checked the local weather and was pleased to find that there was no rain in the forecast and the temperature would be in the low sixties. Not ideal, but hey, it's the McKenzie River.

The sun was trying to peek through an overcast sky as the two pulled into the visitor lot of the Eugene Police Department headquarters. The building was a newer, modern looking building with colorful neon designs decorating the wall separating police car parking from public parking. The small lobby had a few glass enclosed cases displaying old police department uniforms, badges, pictures of previous Police Chiefs and other law enforcement related objects. There was a narrow counter topped by four thick glassed windows through which you could speak to a clerk. There were small openings beneath the windows to exchange documents with the clerks. One wall held an information rack displaying accident report forms, brochures on home safety and other pamphlets. After a short wait in the lobby Victoria Miller appeared and escorted them up to her office on the second floor. She looked to be in her mid-thirties and was very attractive, not at all what Fife and Trotter had expected. Her brown slacks and yellow sweater showed off her trim figure quite nicely. They all stopped in the break room and poured themselves a cup of coffee before heading down the hall past several small detective cubicles and into her diminutive office. There was no sign of clutter. Unlike Fife whose office was in a constant state of chaos, this woman was definitely well organized. Fife noticed a rolled up yoga mat in one corner, no doubt used to relieve stress which was always abundant in their chosen profession. A single rose was perched in a bud vase on one corner of her desk. The other corner held family pictures. One looked to be a son about ten-years-old and the other a husband who could have been a linebacker in the NFL.

"So," Miller asked as the three of them settled into their chairs "What is it that brings the two of you to our beautiful city?"

"Well," Fife began, "how's the fishing on the McKenzie these days?"

Miller tilted her head slightly forward and said, "Really, you came all this way to talk about fishing?"

"Ok forget about fishing," Fife responded. The woman clearly had no idea of what the really important things in life were. "There seems to be some similarities in a case we're working in Colorado and the homicide you're working on here in Eugene. We understand the killer left a note, and the weapon used to kill the victim, at the scene. The same evidence was at our scene. The weapon in Colorado was used in a Chicago homicide, but based on the note left behind we don't think whoever used it in Chicago was the one who used it in Colorado."

"What did the note at your homicide say?" Miller asked.

"It made a reference to our victim's penchant for campaigning against stricter gun control laws," Fife responded.

"Ours was kinda similar," Miller responded. "The killer referenced the fact that the weapon was purchased at an estate sale and no background check was required. Surprisingly the serial number on the gun was intact. I'm having our people try and track it but haven't heard anything back yet. No telling how long it will take. We also managed to pull a partial print off the barrel of the gun. We're hoping it is enough to possibly find a match if it's somewhere in the system.

Trotter leaned forward and sat his coffee on the corner of the desk. "Now, tracking that serial number may be something I can help with," he said. "Our bureaucracy is pretty slow, but tracking serial numbers on guns for some reason gets a fast response."

"Have at it," Miller said as she pulled the note with the serial number on it out of the file and handed it to him. Trotter stepped out of the small office to make the call.

A few minutes later Trotter stepped back into the crowded office. "Got it," he said. "The gun is registered to a Samuel J. Weatherford in Denver. A quick check showed that Mr. Weatherford died four years ago and his widow died just a few months ago. I expect the estate sale was done by a relative of some kind. We're checking on next of kin now and will have an agent contact whoever that may be first thing tomorrow. Hopefully he or she will still be in the Denver area.

"Good work," Fife said as he turned back to the Eugene detective and took a sip of his coffee.

"So, Ms. Miller, what else can you tell us about your case?"

"You can call me Vik, short for Victoria Ms. seems a little to formal for my taste. So, there are a few more notable things. The victim was a lobbyist for the NRA. He was the keynote speaker at a gun conference being held at the Hilton. Apparently Mr. Lobbyist, one Greg Townsend, felt the Hilton was beneath his station in life. He was staying at a new high-end hotel a few blocks away. The rooms cost three or four times what the rooms go for at the Hilton. Whoever killed him managed to smack him a good one in the face before doing him in. He had blood all over his mouth and chin from a heavy nose bleed. It looked like his nose may have been broken in the scuffle. There was also a second blood stain on the bed that isn't a match for the victim. And one other odd thing, there was a towel missing from the guy's room. One theory is that somehow the killer was shot and used the towel to bind the wound. That would account for the second blood type on the bed. We pulled a slug out of the wall that had a trace of blood on it. Based on the angle of projection we're sure it didn't come from our victim. We're still waiting to see if it matches the victim though, just to be certain. We think it will most likely match the second blood type we found on the bed. Also, the second blood type should be able to tell us if it came from a male or female."

"In addition," Miller continued, "A young female hotel employee went to the room to deliver champagne, saw the body and ran out screaming for a supervisor." She stopped talking and looked through a large stack of folders on her desk. "Ah, here it is," she said as she pulled a sheet out of the folder. "The supervisor showed up in time to see a woman quickly making her way towards the exit. The guy called out to her but was ignored. He just figured she didn't hear him and thought no more about it, but he was able to give us a description of the woman. She was about five-three or so, medium build, brunette wearing a tight fitting black and white dress. She never turned around so no one got a look at her face. She could have been the shooter or maybe a witness but vanished before anyone could get there to track her down." The dynamic duo thanked detective Miller for her time and told her they would fill her in on what they learned from the Weatherford woman as soon as they got the information back from the Denver office.

Fife and Trotter checked out early the next morning and headed about twenty miles east of Eugene to spend a few hours on the McKenzie. Fife had booked a late flight back to give them time for fishing. The weather was a little overcast and in the high forties, a little cool for fishing but hey, a man's gotta do what a man's gotta do. Fife figured they had about two hours before heading to the airport for their flight back to Denver. He'd scraped up enough of his old excess gear to outfit Trotter with the minimum things he needed to fly fish. He spent about a half hour with the FBI agent showing him the basics before heading downstream to fish.

Fife made a couple of false casts then softly landed a parachute Adams on the surface of the water. The fly made a flawless, natural drift from right to left in the lazy current right on the edge of faster water. He took a deep breath and scanned the surrounding countryside taking in the beauty of the river before turning his attention back to the wandering fly. The passionate fisherman made a second cast and glanced up river to see a frustrated Trotter up on the bank trying to dislodge his twisted fly line and leader from the lower limbs of a tall fir tree. It looked like a hopeless case that would probably involve a knife and the cutting of some line to free up the tangled mess. He looked back at the Parachute Adams just in time to see a sixteen inch rainbow trout rise to take the appealing fake insect. Fife gave a quick jerk on his rod to set the hook and the battle was on.

A few minutes later Fife was releasing the trophy trout back into the water when Trotter walked up.

"Just got a call back from our guy in Denver. He said the Weatherford woman recalled selling her late father's guns to a woman at the estate sale. She said the woman who purchased them was well dressed, late thirties, about five-four or so and blonde. She gave her name as Wanda Grisham from Castle Rock, Colorado. He checked the Castle Rock address; no one by that name lived there or had ever heard of a

Wanda Grisham. Except for the hair color, sounds a little like the woman who made that quick exit in Detective Miller's case. Nice fish by the way. I managed to catch a fairly large tree with my efforts. Who would have thought fir trees would have an appetite for a parachute what-cha-ma-call-it?"

Fife stepped up out of the water. "Good work, Trotter," he said. "Not on catching the tree, but on getting the information. Looks like we are starting to hone in on a suspect, never would have guessed it might be a woman."

Trotter called Detective Miller and filled her in on the details as they drove to the airport. "Thanks a lot." Miller said after she heard what Trotter had to say. "Also, here's something else we could use some help with. We got a hit on the print we lifted from the gun in the hotel. The thing is it came back as classified. No name or any other information associated with it and no way for us to get to the information. All we know is that it's someone somewhere in the system. I'll send you a copy of the print, maybe you can have better luck finding out who it belongs to. And one last thing, the blood on the slug from the wall matched the second blood type on the bed. It's a woman; ten-to-one says it was the one the hotel guy called out to as she was leaving."

"Probably so," Trotter responded. "We'll do what we can on that print and get back to you, and thanks again for your help and hospitality."

"What about the print?" Fife asked.

Trotter explained the issue with the print to Fife as they drove. "If it's in the system our folks in D.C. should be able to get to it. And get this; Miller said the second blood type in the hotel room belongs to a woman. That pretty much confirms what we were thinking," he said. The fly fishing novice suggested to Fife that they go back to the car dealer employees to see if anyone remembered seeing a woman matching the descriptions from the hotel and the estate sale near the car dealership around the time of Caldwell's demise. "Kind of a long shot," Trotter remarked, "But you never know."

Jack Wilder stood in line behind Fife and Trotter at the coffee bar near the departure gate at the Eugene airport. He bought a Eugene newspaper to read while he sipped his coffee and waited for the flight to Denver where he would make a connection back to D.C. The lead story was the NRA lobbyist murder. While there were no suspects, the police were looking for a woman of interest who had been seen leaving the hotel and were asking the public for help in locating her. Wilder wondered how many homicides the Eugene PD handled in a year, probably not many given the size of the town.

Chapter 21

Fife was in his office with his feet up on his desk reading the morning paper when Trotter came in.

"What, no coffee this time? I may have to file a formal complaint with your supervisor," Fife said as he put the newspaper down and turned to Trotter.

"Sorry boss, running late this morning and didn't have time to pick any up."

"Not to worry, my boy. Let's take a drive out to that car dealership like you suggested and we'll stop for some on the way. So, what have you found out about the print the fine looking Detective Miller gave you?"

"Well, it's an interesting conundrum." Trotter said as they climbed into Fife's cluttered car. "The print is classified and we, the great FBI, can't even access it. We get the same message Miller and her people did. It's marked Classified, Top Secret, Need to Know Only. Apparently we don't need to know. Damndest thing I've ever seen."

"Weird for sure, could it be someone in the witness protection program?"

"Could be I guess. If that's the case it falls under the U.S. Marshall's bailiwick. I've heard that they aren't too generous when it comes to letting that kind of information out.

"Ok, so who does that leave? Could be NSA, CIA or some other alphabet soup agency we don't even know exists."

"You don't suppose someone in our own government is going around assassinating people do you?"

"Not likely but who really knows what the government is up to these days? If we can't identify that print or catch whoever this is soon we may be close to tossing this thing into the great abyss of cold case files."

They parked the car and went into the opulent showroom of the Mercedes dealer. As they stood in the middle of the massive display area Alan Bishop approached them.

"Detective Fife, Agent Trotter, good to see you again. Have you come back to purchase one of our luxury rides?"

"Actually, Mr. Bishop, we have an important follow up question regarding the murder of Mr. Caldwell. Do you recall a woman who may have come into the dealership somewhere around the time Caldwell was killed?" Fife asked.

"Hmm, now that you mention it, there was a woman who came in the day before he was killed. She was very good looking, but wore her sunglasses the whole time. She said she was recently divorced, had a load of cash from the settlement and was looking to buy a luxury car. Apparently her husband ran off with his secretary or something of that nature. She left in a hurry, said she was later for a meeting with her lawyer. I was expecting her to come back but she never did. Too bad, I'm having a slow month and could really use the sale. Are you sure you aren't interested in a Mercedes? I'm sure we could find something that could fit your budget. It doesn't cost anything to go for a test drive."

"Ha," Fife chuckled, "Won't happen in my lifetime on my meager salary. Now Agent Trotter here is a different story. Rumor is that he's loaded with cash, just dripping with money. Those FBI agents make tons of money. He even buys his coffee at Starbucks. But enough about cars for now, what else can you tell us about this mystery woman?

"Well, she was about five-six or so, slender, had dark hair and a great body. As I said, she kept her sunglasses on the whole time she was here. I kept hoping she would take them off but she never did. She seemed pretty self assured, even a little, oh I don't know, smug or arrogant maybe."

"Anything else?"

"Well, there was one thing. She took notice of Mr. Caldwell up in his office. We talked about his gun and the fact that he always had it with him and visible in his shoulder holster."

"Thanks Mr. Bishop, you've been a great help. If you think of anything else please give us a call," Fife replied as he and Trotter headed out the door.

"So, the plot thickens," Trotter said as they drove back downtown. It looks like we have a pretty clear idea of who our prime suspect may be. We have the woman at the estate sale, the woman leaving the hotel in Eugene and the woman at the Mercedes dealership. Three women with very similar descriptions can't be a coincidence."

"No it can't, my fine Feebie friend. And if the print from the hotel in Eugene is in fact her, then just who the hell can she be? And what agency does she work for? And why would a government agency want to knock off a car dealer? My guess is that she's a former government employee, maybe CIA or something out there that we don't even know exists."

Chapter 22

Addison wasn't totally sure where she was headed. She only knew she needed to put as much distance between herself and Eugene, Oregon as quickly as she could. She drove through the night thinking about where she should strike next. She was sure killing the NRA lobbyist and leaving the notes would make some headlines and it would only be a matter of time before the authorities connected her Colorado activities with the Eugene event.

She'd been driving for nearly twenty-two hours with only short stops and catnaps in rest areas. She was feeling exhausted as she pulled into a Motel 6 just off Interstate 80 near North Platte, Nebraska. Her main meals on the road thus far had been Tylenol and coffee. She wasn't sure if the pain from the gunshot wound was diminishing or if her exhaustion had simply pushed the pain aside. The late night clerk was busy watching the David Letterman show on a small TV in the back of the reception area. He turned and looked at her as she came in and held up a finger indicating he would be with her shortly. As the Letterman segment ended and a commercial came on, the indolent clerk slowly rose and approached the counter.

"What can I do for you?" he asked. Addison filled out the registration form using the name Gretta Garbo and paid cash for the room. The lethargic clerk barely looked at the registration form, handed her a room key and went back to watching the antics of the late night comedian.

Addison paused at the doorway of her room and gave a quick look at her surroundings before stepping into the dingy space. She put the Do Not Disturb sign on the door, took a shower and changed the bandage on her wound. It was a little red but no sign of infection. She plopped down on the lumpy bed and slept for seventeen hours straight. Despite the lumps in the bed she woke up refreshed and starving. She dressed and went next door to a Denny's where she bought a newspaper from the stand next to the front door. She went inside, took a seat at a booth in the back that gave her a clear view of the door and ordered the Grand Slam breakfast with extra bacon and a pot of coffee..

She devoured the huge breakfast in short order then leaned back in the booth and sipped her coffee as she scanned the headlines. The world was beginning to take notice of her crusade. The killing of the NRA lobbyist was the headline just below the front page center fold. She noted that the article had come from United Press International which meant it was being picked up by papers all over the country. National coverage was exactly what she was looking for. Now she just needed to think of another high profile target to keep the momentum going. Who should it be? Another lobbyist? NRA headquarters? Then it came to her, a Supreme Court justice, someone who always sided with the NRA. A gun rights advocate of the highest degree. She recalled something she had read about Justice Harold Baker siding with the NRA to cast the deciding vote in a recent case. In addition, Baker was very vocal on gun rights issues anytime he spoke to the media.

She did a quick map search on her phone and figured she was about halfway to Washington, D.C. She paid for her meal and headed East on I-80. She made the 1400 mile drive in just under twenty-two hours of hard driving with little rest. This time she decided to treat herself to better accommodations. It was just after four in the morning when she checked into The Willard InterContinental hotel on Pennsylvania Ave. near the White House. She used a completely new set of credit cards and identification to register at the luxury hotel. She was now Louisa Hazel from Green Bay, Wisconsin.

Addison took a shower then slept for nearly fourteen hours. She woke refreshed and ready for whatever the day would bring. Aside from being Ms. Hazel, she did nothing to change her appearance, no wig or outlandish makeup this time around. She just wanted to look and feel like her old self for awhile.

The pain from her wound was barely noticeable as she pulled back the curtains and looked out her fifth floor window at the city below. She was glad to be in clean, comfortable familiar surroundings for a change. The sun was sinking into the horizon and the lights of the city were slowly blinking to life.

She got dressed, put on a little makeup and made her way downstairs to the elegant Round Robin bar just off the main lobby of the hotel. She took a seat opposite the entry door. There she could watch Washington's elite come and go. A handsome middle aged bartender wearing a snappy vest and bow tie sat a napkin in front of her and said, "What can I get for you, Miss?" She ordered a vodka martini with an extra olive. The debonair bartender took two steps to his left, pulled the necessary ingredients from beneath the bar and skillfully mixed the cocktail. He smiled at her as he set the elegant glass down before heading to the other end of the bar where an impatient, disheveled looking patron in an ill-fitting suit was holding a raised empty pilsner glass.

Jack Wilder spent a good part of the afternoon filling Justice Baker in on the trip he'd made to Eugene and what he'd found out about the CREEPS organization. He told Baker that he thought the threat had been diffused, but advised him to stay vigilant. The busy judge took it all in without making any comments or asking questions. Wilder made no mention of the fact that he had slapped the hapless hippie senseless to get his attention. He simply told Baker who the guy was and what he'd been up to. The Justice seemed to be pleased with the outcome, thanked Jack for his time and wrote him a check for four thousand dollars for services rendered. They'd never discussed the financial arrangement and Jack was more than pleased with the amount. *Hmm,* Wilder thought to himself, *maybe I've found my new calling....Jack Wilder Private Investigator.*

After leaving the Judge, Jack felt a minor celebration was in order and pulled into the valet parking area of the Willard Intercontinental. The Round Robin bar was one of his old favorite D.C. haunts in between CIA assignments. He enjoyed sitting in the bar and listening to the political windbags tell each other about their highly embellished accomplishments. Jack handed his keys to the valet and walked across the ornate lobby to the famous bar. As he entered he felt like he had taken a step back in time. There she was sitting at the bar, Addison Cooper, looking more stunning than ever.

The last time he'd seen the beautiful spy they were taking a class at Langley together on the Barrett M98B sniper rifle. They had taken turns becoming efficient at using the killing machine. One would be the spotter while the other would be the shooter. They started out with targets at 100 yards, then 500 and finally 1,000 yards. Although the weapon was capable of making much longer shots, the agency figured most ops would be a 1,000 yards or less. When you are in the CIA and bored out of your mind in between assignments you check the class schedule each week to see what's being offered. There was everything from parachuting to poisoning. Agents would take classes to add to their list of skills. When an operation came up, the agency would check the data base to see who had the skills needed to complete the operation.

There'd been a rumor floating around that Addison had been killed in a Middle East operation gone bad. Jack was pleased to see that she appeared to be alive and well.

"Hello, Addison," he said as he took the empty stool next to her at the bar. "It's great to see you. I heard rumors that you were no longer among the living."

"Well I'll be damned, if it isn't Jack Wilder. I'd heard the same about you." *Oh crap!* Addison thought to herself, *First I see him in Oregon and now here.* "So Jack, are you still with the Company?"

"Actually no, I left about a year ago, how about you?"

"I left too, nearly seven years ago."

"So seven years, what have you been up to since you left, married, kids?"

"Widowed, one son six years old killed in a school shooting by a lunatic with a huge cache of weapons. Somehow he slipped through the system. I'm telling you Jack, it's too easy for people to get their hands on guns these days and the lawmakers just stick their collective heads in the sand while they keep taking millions from NRA lobbyists."

Jack waved the bartender over and ordered a beer, then took a handful of peanuts from an ornate glass dish on the bar and popped them into his mouth while he tried to think of something meaningful to say. He put his hand on her shoulder foolishly thinking his touch would somehow bring her some comfort.

"I don't know what to say. I can't even begin to imagine how you must feel. I mean losing a husband and a child. Life just isn't supposed to be like that."

"It's not about how I feel, Jack. It's about how this whole damn country should feel. Something has to be done to get the people to act. The NRA needs to have some of their power taken away and don't get me started on Congress and the judicial system. Those greedy bastards only exacerbate the problem by taking millions from the NRA thugs while they turn a blind eye to their constituency. Did you see where that moron Supreme Court guy Harold Baker recently sided with the NRA and their stupid second amendment argument? Do you think a six year old at school gives a crap about the Second Amendment? His name was Joey and I had an erroneous expectation that school was a safe place for him. I was wrong Jack. There is no safe place anywhere for anyone to be anymore. The case Baker sided with the NRA on was something about a state's ban on assault rifles and high capacity magazines. Why does anybody need a high capacity magazine outside of a war zone?" Jack opened his mouth to say something about Justice Baker, but thought better of it and simply took a sip of his beer. He was beginning to worry about where the conversation was headed. He really hadn't ever given any thought to gun laws and the Second Amendment. After all, he'd made his living using various weapons for the last several years. Guns were simply one of the tools of his trade.

Jack made an effort to steer the conversation in a different direction. "So, what made you decide to leave the agency?" he asked.

"A rocket-propelled grenade through the windshield of the Humvee I was riding in. It killed several good marines as well as the woman I was escorting out of the country. I spent six months in the hospital and had several operations to get back on my feet. But enough about me Jack, what I'm talking about here is something much more important. Did you know that since 2009 there have been over 130 mass shootings and 50 of those were in schools?" Addison took a deep breath, swallowed the rest of her martini and held her glass up to ask the bartender for a refill. "I'm telling you Jack something has to be done. They're killing our kids. The people in this country need to wake up! Those bastards totally ruined my life. I had it all, a loving husband, a beautiful child and a charming New England cottage. It was the life I dreamed of when I was a little girl."

"Just who are those bastards?"

"Christ Jack, pay attention! I'm talking about all of them, Congress, the NRA, Harold Baker and the rest of his Supreme Court conservative buddies. All of them. Something has to be done to get their attention."

"But aren't you talking about closing the barn door after the horse has already gotten out? It's not like the government can go around and take everyone's guns away."

"You see that's the problem Jack. Anytime anyone talks about gun control, the NRA and conservative members of Congress shout they're trying to take away your guns. That's total bullshit. No one is going to take away the guns that are already out there. No one has ever said let's round up all the guns. Sensible people are simply calling for sensible actions like more thorough background checks and limits on the number of rounds in a magazine, a thorough training course on the use and safety of guns before you are allowed to buy one. It's all just simple common sense." She took another deep breath and a gulp of her fourth martini." Her eyes were drooping a little and she was beginning to slur her words a bit.

"So, what are you thinking needs to be done to get their attention?"

"I really don't know, but it has to be something big. Obviously mass shootings don't get their attention. Maybe somebody needs to blow up NRA headquarters, or the Supreme Court, or maybe even Congress. Get rid of all of them and start over," she said as she swayed a little on her bar stool.

That's when it hit him like a runaway freight train. *She's right, I haven't been paying attention.* His mind flashed back to the article he'd read in the

Eugene airport about the NRA lobbyist being killed in his hotel room. *She was the woman I saw coming out of the Hilton as I was going in! She killed the NRA lobbyist in Eugene.*

"Wait here a minute Jack," she said. "I'm going to the ladies' room." Jack stood, helped her off the bar stool and pointed her towards the ladies' room. He could tell she really had to focus to walk a straight line. He sat back down and finished the last of the one and only beer he had ordered that night. Fifteen minutes later when she hadn't returned Jack asked a woman patron to go in and check on her. The woman came back and told Jack there was no one in the ladies' room. *Damn,* he thought, *where the hell has she gone, and what is she going to do? Was she crazy enough to blow up NRA headquarters or was she going after the Supreme Court or maybe just Harold Baker?* He checked at the front desk to see if she was registered at the hotel. The desk clerk assured him there was no one named Addison Cooper or any other Addison registered as a guest of the hotel.

Jack returned to the bar, ordered another beer and tried to concentrate on what he should do. Should he call Baker or maybe call the NRA? He was positive Addison had killed the NRA lobbyist in Eugene. On the other hand, she was right about a lot of what she'd said. Maybe he should just leave it alone and let the chips fall where they may, although he knew he couldn't. He needed to find out just who Addison Cooper was these days, where she had been the last several years and what she was planning to do. It was time to call Barry "The Wonder Boy" Godly again. He knew Barry could put together a chronology of what Addison Cooper had been up to.

Chapter 23

A cold rain was falling from a dark grey sky when Ballinger's plane from France touched down at Baltimore Washington International airport. The killer had an angular face, stood a little over six feet tall and weighed a solid 220. With scant body fat and muscles reinforced by steroids, Ballinger could have passed as a wide receiver for the Dallas Cowboys. He had spent time in Iraq as a Marine sniper killing bad guys for his country. Now he spent time killing anyone if the price was high enough. His last target had been an OPEC analyst in Vienna. He'd been hired by an obscenely wealthy and corrupt U.S. Senator who was now doing thirty to life for arranging the hit on the analyst. The unfortunate OPEC employee had been on the verge of exposing the Senator's corrupt association with several OPEC ministers to create a false oil shortage. Ballinger had a subsequent falling out with the Senator and was instrumental in the politico's downfall. He'd sent incriminating videos of the Senator discussing his role in the murder to Jack Wilder. Wilder and the FBI had subsequently taken the Senator down. Ballinger was not the kind of guy you could do battle with and expect to come out on top.

Ballinger made his way through the crowds to the car rental area where he used one of his many alias credit cards to rent a luxury Cadillac. He negotiated the busy traffic getting out of the airport, jumped on I-95 West, merged onto the Baltimore Washington

Parkway and headed to one of his favorite D.C. haunts. The rain had increased and the rush hour traffic crept along at a speedy fifteen miles an hour as he made his way to The City Tavern Club in Georgetown. Originally built in 1796 as an inn and tavern, it was a major hub of civic life. George Washington, Thomas Jefferson and their contemporaries were often seen in the tavern discussing the politics of the day. It was here in the comfort of a cozy chair in front of a large stone fireplace that Ballinger would drink 18 year-old scotch and plan the details of his current assignment. His contact in Brussels had sent him a complete package on his target, Supreme Court Justice Harold Baker. This would be the highest profile hit he'd ever made. The package included several pictures of Baker, his home phone and address as well as his gym where he worked out and the various clubs and organizations he belonged to in the area. Most useful to Ballinger however, was the schedule of events Baker would attend in the next couple of weeks. He perused the schedule and focused on a fundraising event at the Kennedy Center where the Justice would be giving a speech. It was the kind of event where various high profile dignitaries would no doubt arrive in chauffeured limousines. Washington's elite would show off their wealth and power as they stumbled over each other clamoring for publicity and photo ops.

There was a time when Ballinger was a true patriot and would never have killed any American civilians. That all changed in 2008 when he was a

Marine serving in Afghanistan. He'd been assigned to a squad in the Kunar Province near the Pakistan border. He had no sniper duties that day and had been assigned to work with some Afghan forces when a battle broke out. The first thing he did was call for air cover and reinforcements. Despite repeated calls for air support, it never arrived. Field commanders deemed it to be too close to civilian populations. He watched as three fellow Marines and ten Afghan security force members, one by one, lost their lives in the heated battle. One brave helicopter pilot finally defied orders and landed to evacuate Ballinger and the other remaining wounded Marine. The wounded soldier died on the operating table a few hours later. The rest of the bodies were recovered the next day. Lives lost that day could have been saved if the commanders in the safe confines of their air conditioned huts had responded to his call. Ballinger vowed to never again depend on anyone for help when things got tough. From that day forward the only life he cared about was his own and the only one he trusted was himself.

Ballinger took another sip of his expensive scotch and sank lower into the soft leather chair as he stared at the crackling fire. He just needed to figure out how he was going to be driving the limousine that would pick Baker up to attend the fundraising event at the Kennedy Center.

Early the next morning Ballinger was parked a block away from Baker's house. He was a little surprised to see Baker picked up by a limousine. This was out of the ordinary even for a Supreme Court justice. Then he remembered Baker's wealth and it made sense. Why would someone that rich want to deal with the stress of Washington traffic when he could pay someone else to deal with the blaring horns and crazy drivers. Plus it would give him the opportunity to get some work done during the lengthy commute. He followed the limo from Baker's house to the Supreme Court building. Then he followed the limo back to its place of business on I street not far from Georgetown. He watched as the tall Hispanic looking driver parked the prestigious vehicle and went inside. Ballinger parked in a customer slot in front of the building and went inside where he was greeted by a energetic young lady behind the counter. The bubbly clerk looked up and said, "Hi, welcome to Fancy Rides. How can I be of service?"

"I was just wondering if you ever rent limousines out long term. My company has a bid out on a large project that may require me to be in the area for six months or so. I would like to be picked up from my hotel, dropped off at work, then picked up at work and dropped back at the hotel."

"Oh that wouldn't be a problem at all," the young woman replied. "We do exactly that same thing for one of the Supreme Court justices. We even make sure he always has the same driver." She handed him a rate sheet that explained all the various cost options.

"Thanks very much. This is exactly what I was looking for. If we get the contract I will be back in touch," Ballinger said as he turned and headed for the door. He glanced past the reception counter into the driver's lounge to get a good look at Baker's driver as he turned. A little after six that evening Ballinger was parked a block away from Fancy Rides where he watched as Baker's driver parked the limo, got into a red Toyota and headed for home. Ballinger made a U turn and pulled in behind the Toyota as it passed him.

Jorge Padilla was an illegal immigrant who came to the U.S. with his parents when he was only three years old. They made the eleven hundred mile trek from Mexico City to El Paso in the back of a 1953 Chevy pickup along with seven chickens and a pig. Jorge's uncle, who was driving the truck, pulled into an alley in Juarez about three miles from the border. It was there that he covered the family with an old tarp and several bales of hay before driving to the border crossing. As the truck pulled to a stop at the border crossing his uncle handed the U.S. border guard an egg carton containing two thousand dollars, payment to insure the truck would not be searched. The portly guard thanked his Uncle for the eggs and waved the truck filled with illegals and the barnyard critters through.

Like many others before them, the Padillas followed the farm harvests, working in fields and living in various states of squalor along the way. It was in one of those migrant camps where Jorge, at the tender age of seventeen, met and fell in love with Sarita Gomez. Sarita and her family had only recently arrived in the U.S., also illegally. Leaving their families behind, the young couple made their way to Florida following the orange grove harvest. Tired of the back breaking work, the couple eventually worked their way north to the suburbs of Washington D.C. where Sarita landed a job as a hotel maid and Jorge was hired on as a Fancy Rides minion. It was there that Jorge helped maintain the fleet of limousines. He did everything from helping change the oil to washing and waxing the luxury rides eventually working his way up to driving a $75,000 Lincoln Federal Silverstone limo as Justice Baker's permanent chauffeur.

Jorge and his family lived in a modest neighborhood in Edmonston, Maryland, about 20 miles Northeast of Georgetown. Their house was one of the many older homes in the area with small, well-kept yards and mature landscaping. Most residents of the neighborhood were young, middle class working families. Jorge and Sarita were one of the few families in the area who were rented. Their dream was to someday own such a nice house. The biggest obstacle was their illegal immigrant status. Any kind of loan application would most likely reveal their status as illegal aliens.

Ballinger parked a block away and watched as two young children playing in the front yard jumped to their feet and ran to meet Jorge as he pulled into the short driveway of the modest home. The small yard was well-kept with neatly trimmed grass and a row of shrubs that lined either side of the sidewalk leading to the petite front porch. A short, moderately plump Hispanic woman stood in the doorway wiping her hands on the colorful apron she wore as she watched the children run to greet their father. She was no doubt finishing up making a fine traditional dinner for her family of four. The faint smell of freshly made tortillas pierced the air. When the door closed with all the family headed in for dinner, Ballinger drove slowly past their humble home and made note of the name on the mail box, Padilla. Jorge Padilla didn't know it, but he was destined to meet Ballinger in the very near future.

The next day Ballinger sat in his rental a block down from the limo driver's house with his camera and zoom lens. He took several pictures of Mrs. Padilla as she handed the kids lunch sacks and gave each one a hug and a kiss on their way out the door. He watched as the two Padilla children ran down the street to meet their friends at the school bus stop. He took several pictures of both kids playing with their friends as they waited for the bus. He followed the big yellow transport to the school and took several more pictures as the two hopped off the bus and ran up the steps into Carson Elementary school. When he had all the pictures he needed he called the Padilla house from his car.

"Hello Mrs. Padilla, this is Frank Holland from D.C. Transportation Services. We provide the school bus service for Carson Elementary School. We're doing a survey to see if we need to add more buses or make any adjustments to our routes for Carson Elementary as well as some of the other schools we serve." Ballinger was using a concept called social engineering. By making calls using a bogus name and asking what seemed like innocent questions a person can gather a lot of useful information."So, the first question is, do you have children who attend Carson Elementary?"

"Yes we have two children who attend Carson."

"And what grades are they in?"

"Jose is in the third grade; he's eight years old and his sister, Carmelita, is in the fifth grade and she's ten-years old."

Now Ballinger had exactly what he was looking for, the children's names and ages. He asked a few more questions that would seem relevant, thanked Mrs. Padilla for her time and hung up. After a few more days of surveillance Ballinger had all the information he needed.

As it turned out, Jorge Padilla had coffee every morning at seven o'clock with some of his friends at a coffee shop near Fancy Rides. Padilla was always the first to arrive, usually fifteen minutes or so before the rest of the gang began drifting in. The group usually spent close to an hour drinking coffee and catching up on the latest events in their lives before breaking up and heading off to their various jobs.

Ballinger arrived at a little after 6 a.m. and took a seat in the back of the coffee shop where Padilla and his friends congregated. He ordered a light breakfast of oatmeal, toast and coffee as he waited for Padilla to show up. He'd just finished his breakfast when Padilla came through the door and took a seat at the group's usual table. Ballinger dropped a ten dollar bill on the table, picked up his coffee and joined Padilla at his table. "Excuse me, do I know you?" Padilla asked as Ballinger took a seat.

"Mr. Padilla, I have a dilemma," Ballinger began as he took a sip of his coffee. "Here's the thing, I need to borrow the limo you'll be using to drive Justice Baker to his fund raiser this Friday evening."

"What? You must be out of your mind Dude. There ain't no way I'm gonna give you that limo. Wait a minute…. did one of my friends put you up to this? They did, didn't they?" Padilla smiled and looked around expecting to see some of his friends standing nearby laughing at the practical joke they'd played on him. He scanned the entire restaurant looking for a familiar smiling face. Seeing none he turned back to the pushy stranger. Padilla had a puzzled look on his face while the stranger's face held a cold, hard, menacing stare.

"I need that limo "*Dude*" and you're going to bring it to me."

At this point Padilla's puzzlement began to turn to anger.

"Hold on there, homey," Padilla said. " Just who the hell do you think you are coming in here like some big time mafia guy or something telling me what I got to do and what I don't got to do? You need to go away and bother someone else." Ballinger took a casual sip of his coffee and reached into his pocket. He pulled out a picture of the older Padilla child and laid it on the table. He could see the instant fear appear in the young father's eyes.

"I'll tell you who I am," Ballinger said as he laid a second picture on the table. This one was the kids getting off the school bus. "I'm the guy with the power to eliminate your whole family with a simple phone call." Padilla's face turned pale as he looked at the pictures of his kids. The waitress appeared with a pot of coffee and topped off Ballinger's cup then turned to Padilla. "Are you okay sugar? You look kinda pale." Padilla forced himself to give her a polite smile. "Just a little indigestion," he said, as she put a cup down on the table in front of him and filled it with coffee. "Oh, I'm sorry," the kindly waitress replied. "I hope you get to feeling better soon," she said as she turned and headed for another table.

"What are you doing with pictures of my kids?" an agitated Padilla whispered as he leaned into the table and looked directly at the stranger.

"An associate of mine took them," Ballinger lied. "Here's one of your lovely wife too," he said, as he laid another picture on the table. "You have a beautiful family Mr. Padilla. I believe the kids are eight and ten years old and I'm sure you want them to grow up and give you many grandchildren don't you? It would certainly be a shame to see anything happen to them wouldn't it?" Ballinger calmly took another sip of coffee and looked directly at Padilla. He could see the panic in the man's eyes. "Now, here's what you're going to do for me if you don't want to see your family get hurt," he said as he gathered all the pictures into a stack, tapped them on the table and put them back in his pocket. "On Friday afternoon at exactly three o'clock you're going to meet me here with the limo. I will get in it and drive away. You will stay here or go anyplace you want except home. A little after eight that evening I will return and give the limo back to you and our business will be concluded. You'll be free to go home to your beautiful family." Ballinger paused and looked around the restaurant, carefully taking in his surroundings. He turned his attention back to the frightened limo driver and leaned closer to him. "Comprende amigo?" he said to Padilla.

"Yes, but why?" Padilla replied.

"You don't get to ask questions my friend, you just get to do as you're told. If you go home anytime before eight, or if you go to the police, you'll never see your family again. If you do as instructed you will find your family safe and sound when you go home and you will never see or hear from me again." Ballinger stood to leave and put his hand on Padilla's shoulder. "Everything will be fine as long as you follow my instructions. As you can see, we can get to

181

your family anytime, so don't do anything foolish. See you Friday."

As Ballinger left Padilla looked down at his shaking hands, took a deep breath and tried to calm his frayed nerves. He knew he had no choice. On Friday he would deliver the limo to the stranger as instructed.

Chapter 24

Addison woke feeling the effects of the six or seven martinis she'd consumed the night before while visiting with her old CIA friend. It had been years since she had downed liquor in those quantities. The most she and Morgan ever drank was a small glass of wine with dinner, and then only on special occasions. Her head was telling her to take some aspirin, her stomach was churning like a cement mixer and the light coming through the curtains was mounting a blinding assault on her sensitive bloodshot eyes. She slowly got out of bed and made her way to the bathroom where she splashed cold water on her face and looked at her reflection in the mirror. Her hair and makeup were beyond a mess. She felt like all she needed to complete her disheveled look was a broomstick to ride away on. As the haze in her mind slowly began to lift, she tried to recall her conversation with Jack Wilder. Had she said too much to her old colleague in her rant against the lack of gun controls in the U.S.? She knew Wilder was smart but hopefully not smart enough to figure out what she was up to. At any rate, there was nothing she could do about it even if he did put it all together. The only thing to do now was continue to move forward with her plan.

Addison took a shower which made her feel a bit better. She put on her dark sunglasses and grabbed a cup of coffee and a muffin from the espresso stand in the lobby on her way out of the hotel. She hailed a cab for the short ride to the Supreme Court building. Traffic was light as the cabbie maneuvered his way down Pennsylvania to Constitution, turned onto First Street and parked in front of the Supreme Court building. The trip took less than ten minutes. It would've been an easy walk for someone not suffering the residual effects of several martinis. She paid the driver, walked up the steps and took a seat on a bench next to the flag pole. She finished her muffin and coffee as she stared up at the portico of eight massive Corinthian columns providing the monumental entrance to the highest court in the land.

The huge flag began to billow as a cold breeze made its way through the spacious courtyard. Addison turned up her coat collar and fell in line behind several tourists making their way inside. They all placed their belongings on the x-ray conveyor under the watchful eyes of a stern looking security guard. The guard asked each person in line if they were carrying any guns, knives or other weapons. One old guy from Grand Rapids, Michigan was turned away because he volunteered the fact that he was carrying a small penknife with a three inch blade.

Addison wandered through the massive hallways of the great building taking in the statues, pictures, the great spiral staircase and historical notes offered in a variety of places. She struck up a conversation with one of the security guys and was able to find out that eight of the nine judicial chambers were located on the second floor and the ninth was on the third floor. After carefully studying the layout it became clear that it would be nearly impossible to kill Baker while he was in the building. A few days earlier she'd taken a cab to the Georgetown neighborhood where the Justice lived and decided she couldn't take him out at home either. The streets were narrow with little parking and the houses were all very close together with small, hard to get to, back yards. She got the feeling that most of the neighbors spent a lot of time looking out their windows. As she walked around she saw people peeking through windows to see who was walking by. She didn't want to take a chance on having to run through this kind of neighborhood.

She returned to her hotel, fired up her laptop and began to research Justice Baker more thoroughly. She learned all about his judicial history and was able to peruse his opinions on several of the cases that had been decided by the nine justices. In addition to his staunch support of the NRA, Baker also broadly supported companies that had been sued for various environmental issues. Addison became more determined that the guy needed to go. To her surprise, she saw that he was scheduled to attend a fundraiser at the Kennedy Center later that week. As she thought about it she decided that would be the best place for the hit. Lots of people and probably very little security unless the President was planning to attend which wasn't likely since he was reportedly vacationing in Hawaii for the next week.

Addison pulled up a map on Google Earth and studied the area around the Kennedy Center. Several buildings looked like they could provide height and cover to set up a sniper nest. The next morning she dressed in jeans and a sweater, put on a blonde wig and took a cab to the Kennedy Center where she spent two hours walking around the area. She wore large dark sunglasses to further hide her features as she explored the neighborhood. The Columbia Plaza apartments sat directly across the street from the drop off zone at the Kennedy Center and adjacent to the Foggy Bottom campus of George Washington University. Columbia Plaza held a plethora of boutique shops, the kind you would expect to find in most any university district in the country. She stopped in Casey's Coffee Shop around the corner from the main apartment entrance and ordered a cup of coffee to go.

She carried the cup to the leasing office of the apartment complex and sat patiently in a well decorated waiting area while the plump manager explained the no pet policy to a potential new tenant. When the well dressed woman finished up with the couple she turned to Addison and asked how she could be of service. When Addison saw the woman's make up she nearly burst out laughing. The overuse of rouge on her chubby cheeks brought to mind a circus clown. Addison asked to see an apartment on the highest floor available that faced the Potomac River. She carefully studied the surroundings as the manager took her to see the only unit available on the fifth floor that faced the river. When they reached the top floor Addison glanced down the hall and saw exactly what she was looking for, the access ladder to the roof. After viewing the luxury apartment Addison thanked the manager for her time, told her she would give it some consideration and left.

In the cab ride back to the hotel she thought about what Wilder had said about closing the barn door after the horse had already left. *Was she wasting her time? Would her actions really make any kind of difference or was she just seeking some kind of revenge for her son's murder? No, something had to be done. People needed to understand what was happening in their world and who was responsible. Somehow Congress had forgotten that they were representatives of the people who elected them, not the NRA or any of the hundreds of lobbyists that constantly prowled the halls of the nation's capital with buckets of money to purchase favors.* She had started down this road and vowed to see it through to the end, whatever that end might be.

She glanced out the window and looked up at the sky. It was a dull gray much like most of her life had been the last few weeks. She saw the elegant headstones of a cemetery they were passing and wondered how long it would be before she was lying in a grave somewhere. The more she thought about it the more she thought it was the only way her quest could end. She thought of Morgan and Joey and wondered about God and heaven. *Was there a God? Was there a heaven? Was what she was doing something that would get her into heaven or would she be headed in the opposite direction? If there were a God, why had he taken Morgan and Joey so soon?* Tears ran down her cheeks as she stared out at the bleakness of the day. She'd just finished drying her eyes when the cab pulled up in front of the hotel.

Chapter 25

Jack took a seat in the lobby of the Willard Intercontinental Hotel. He was hoping that Addison was staying in the hotel under an alias and would, at some point, come through the lobby. It was a long shot but at this point a long shot was all he had to work with. He picked a newspaper up from a coffee table and perused through it while he scanned the area for any sign of Addison. He'd only been there a short while when his cell phone vibrated in his pocket. Barry was calling.

"So what did you find out kid?" Jack asked as he took the call.

"Some pretty interesting stuff. To begin with, she wasn't killed in the Middle East as a lot of people thought. She was there though on a very deep covert mission. She was escorting a warlord's wife back to the U.S. for interrogation. The wife was supposedly going to give up some vital information on Al Qaeda operations." Jack could hear Barry slurp one of his energy drinks as the kid paused to take a breath. "The op went south on the way out. The convoy was hit and a lot of people were killed including several Marines. Addison was apparently sitting next to the woman they were bringing out when their vehicle was hit by an RPG. The woman informant was killed instantly and Addison was somehow blown free of the Humvee. She ended up in critical condition and got a quick trip back to the states. She spent a month at Walter Reed and then she was transferred to a private hospital. It took six months and several operations to put the lady back together."

"Hmm. Okay she's alive at that point, then what?"

"She took a medical retirement and moved to New Hampshire where she married a guy named Morgan Wright. She kept her maiden name of Cooper. They had one kid, a boy named Joey. Morgan died of a rapid growing cancer and Joey was killed in a school shooting at the age of six. And that was only the beginning of her bad luck. Shortly after the son was killed her house blew up and burned to the ground. She was apparently killed in the explosion. Now here's the interesting thing. No body was ever recovered. Local authorities are stumped. The family car was in the garage and nearly melted. They were able to confirm the plates and model though, and it was the car that belonged to Addison. There was no record of any cab company picking her up before the explosion. If she just walked away no one saw her leave. So, everyone involved seems pretty sure she was in the house when it blew. They just can't come up with an explanation as to why there wasn't a body in what was left of the house. Speculation is that the fire was so hot the body would have been totally cremated."

Jack listened to it all then closed his eyes and rubbed his forehead with the tips of his fingers. He knew Addison was alive and well and was ninety-nine percent certain she'd killed the NRA lobbyist in

Eugene. He thanked Barry for his help, said he would be in touch if he needed anything else and hung up. He sat the newspaper on his lap and looked around the hotel lobby hoping to see Addison somewhere.

After sitting for two hours with nothing to show for it Jack gave up, went out to the street and hailed a cab. Just as his cab pulled away from the curb a second cab dropped off a single passenger. It was Addison. "Stop," Jack shouted at the driver. Before his cab was completely stopped Jack jumped out and tossed the driver a twenty dollar bill."Keep the change," he said as he sprinted back to the hotel lobby.

He got to the middle of the lobby just in time to see the doors close as Addison stepped toward the back of the elevator. Jack could see that there were only two other people in that elevator. He watched as the numbers above the elevator lit up marking the location of the elevator as it ascended. It stopped on the ninth and eleventh floors before returning to the lobby level. As the doors opened Jack got on the empty elevator and punched the button for the ninth floor. He didn't expect to see Addison standing there waiting for him when he arrived but he did see a maid with a cleaning cart parked in front of an empty room one door down from the elevator. "Excuse me," he said. "Did you see the people who got off this elevator a couple of minutes ago?"

"Yes, I did," she replied, "but it wasn't people, it was just one person, a very pretty lady."

191

"Did you see which room she went into?"

"We are not supposed to tell people the room numbers of our guests." Jack opened his wallet and pulled out a twenty-dollar bill. The maid cast a nervous glance up and down the hallway.

"It's okay," Jack said as he retrieved a second twenty from his wallet. "I'm a friend of hers." The maid took the money from Jack's outstretched hand and said, "I'm sorry sir, I can't help you." She began pushing her cart toward the end of the hall. She hesitated three doors down from the elevator and tilted her head towards the door before continuing on her way.

Addison had just finished changing her clothes when she heard the knock at the door. She looked through the peep hole to see Wilder standing there. She held her breath and stood perfectly still hoping he would go away. After a few minutes and a second knock she heard him say "Come on Addison, I know you're there. I saw you get into the elevator a little bit ago." She opened the door then turned and walked back into the room taking a seat in one of the side chairs next to the round table sitting in the corner of the room. Jack followed her in and took a seat on the opposite side of the table.

"So Wilder, we meet again," she said as she leaned towards him and met his eyes with hers. A short staring contest ensued as she waited for him to make the first move.

Jack drummed his fingers on the table, took a deep breath and said, "So, are you sure you know what you're doing?"

"Know what I'm doing? I have no idea what you're talking about Jack."

"Addison, I saw you in Eugene that night. You were coming out of the Hilton in an obvious hurry while I was going in. We passed each other. I'm sure it was the same night you killed the NRA lobbyist." He drummed his fingers on the table again. "After our conversation the other night I don't see how you could deny it."

"Well I am denying it Jack. I've never been to Eugene and I certainly didn't kill any NRA lobbyist. Just what gives you the right to come in here, uninvited I might add, and start making outrageous accusations?"

"Cut the crap, Addison. I'm not buying it. We were in Looking Glass together. I know what your training was and what you're capable of."

"You don't know anything Jack. You don't know the pain of losing a husband to cancer. You don't know the pain of losing a child, a small innocent child killed while he was at school by a lunatic with a gun, a lunatic with several guns. He was at school when he was killed Jack, at school! He was only six years old. I can never hold him again or take him to school or pick him up when he falls over on his bicycle. Kids are supposed to be safe at school Jack. Crazy people with guns aren't supposed to be there running the halls and killing people. Crazy people aren't supposed to be able to get guns, but they do." She stood and began to pummel him with her fists as a river of tears streamed down her beautiful face. He did nothing to stop her. He knew it wasn't him she was attacking. If it were, her actions would be much more lethal. She was attacking the bottled up pain and anger she'd been carrying. When she finally stopped, he wrapped his arms around her and held her close until the waterworks came to an end. He kissed her on the cheek, turned and walked out the door.

Chapter 26

Wilder waited a day, and then went back to the hotel to find Addison. A hotel maid was just coming out of Addison's room as he approached the door. He peeked in the door at the empty room. "Excuse me," he said to the maid. "Do you know how long ago the lady in this room left?"

"No Señor I do not," she replied. She closed the door firmly behind her. "They say room ready to clean, so here I am. I cleaning room. Lady must be check out already." With that the maid just shrugged and shook her head as she pushed her cart down the hall toward the next empty room. As she pushed the towel laden trolley down the long corridor Jack heard her say "I can't clean room if peoples keep asking me question all day."

"Damn it!" Jack said to himself as he walked back down the hall and pushed the button for the elevator. He knew he had to figure out what Addison was up to, and he had a sinking feeling that whatever she was planning would be happening soon. He went down to the bar, ordered a beer and started piecing together all that she had said to him. "All of them" she had said, "Congress, the NRA, Harold Baker and the rest of his Supreme Court conservative buddies." He thought about it for awhile. Okay, she'd killed the NRA lobbyist in Eugene so that basically left Congress, Harold Baker and the rest of the conservative element on the Supreme Court. Jack took a sip of his beer and grabbed a handful of peanuts as the gears started turning in his head. *Can't kill all of Congress or even the whole Supreme Court, for that matter. Both, too big and too well guarded. Although if she had a plan to do in all of Congress I'd probably sign up to help her. That leaves Baker, he's the one she mentioned by name and he's the one I'm supposed to be protecting.*

Jack pulled out his cell phone and rang Baker's number at the Supreme Court. His secretary answered, "Justice Baker's office, how may I help you?"

"Jack Wilder calling for Justice Baker."

Baker came on the line. "Hello Mr. Wilder, what's up?"

"Well Judge, I have come across some information that makes me think you may still be in someone's sights."

"Nonsense, didn't you set those hippie bastards in Oregon straight?"

"I did sir, but this information comes from a different source and points to someone else."

"Well, tell me, do you have anything concrete to go on?"

"Not exactly, at least not yet, it's more of a gut instinct based on experience."

"Listen Jack, I have had lots of threats over the years and the only one that really seemed credible was the one from that group in Oregon that you've already dealt with. So, if you can't offer anything of real substance, I need to get back to work. Call me back if you find anything concrete." With that the line went dead.

Baker turned to his secretary and said," It was that Wilder fellow. I paid him a small fortune to check on one of the death threats and now I think he is trying to make stuff up to come after some more money. It's not going to work."

"Hmm, "Jack thought *"what a bozo. He's thinks pretty highly of himself; hope he has a lot of life insurance. "* Jack knew he and Addison had pretty much the same training early in their respective careers at the CIA. She would probably make an attempt on the good Justice's life, but how and where would she do it?

When Jack first met with Baker he'd asked a lot of questions and taken notes. What was Baker's schedule for the next month or so? What was his usual route to and from the Supreme Court? Could he think of any specific cases he'd ruled on that might give reason for threats against his life? Could he recall any enemies from previous judicial cases or colleagues from law school that may have held a grudge? Jack pulled these notes from his pocket and began to review them as he sipped his beer. He focused on Baker's schedule where he saw the good judge was scheduled to give a brief speech at a fundraiser on Friday at the Kennedy Center. *That's it. The perfect opportunity to take the guy out.*

Jack thought back his early days at the CIA and recalled the sniper training he and Addison had gone through together. He wondered how often Addison may have put that training to use during her career with the CIA. He had used it a time or two in his own stint at the Company. Jack stuffed the notes back in his pocket, threw a twenty on the bar and headed for the door. He hailed a cab and headed to the Kennedy Center for the Performing Arts.

Jack got out of the cab and scanned the surrounding area looking for the best sniper vantage point. Height and distance were key ingredients for a clear shot and speedy escape. He quickly picked out the nearby Columbia Plaza apartments. The rooftop of the complex provided plenty of height and cover to set up a sniper shot and it was directly across from the drop off point at the Kennedy Center. Jack walked into the manager's office of the luxury apartment complex and was greeted by the bubbly overweight and overly madeup Stella Winkler. Jack explained that he and his wife had just moved into the area and were looking for a place with a view. "Oh, that must have been your wife that was in yesterday," Stella said as she fished the keys out of a drawer for the units on the fifth floor. "Could've been," Jack replied, "what did she look like?" *Bingo, she's been here."*

"Slender, blonde hair and very attractive."

"Yup, that's her. I wasn't sure I was in the right place. She told me about where it was but I'm terrible with directions. She seemed pretty excited about the unit you showed her and told me to come have a look at it."

Jack followed Stella as she turned left out of the elevator and headed down the hall. He noted the ladder at the end of the hallway leading to the roof. As he left he told Stella the apartment was very impressive and they'd most likely be back in touch in a few days.

Jack spent the next hour walking around the neighborhood getting the lay of the land. He didn't know where Addison was at the moment but he was pretty sure he knew where she'd be on Friday.

Chapter 27

Dark clouds were rolling in from the west as Ballinger sat in his car across the street from the coffee shop where Padilla would soon arrive with the limo. The small eatery was surprisingly busy at that hour. He watched as an elderly man and woman left the establishment and looked up at the ominous sky. The guy looked older than dirt and was wearing an old pair of dark gray slacks pulled up about six inches above his slender waist. He had on a red and yellow plaid shirt buttoned all the way up to the collar. An ancient looking overcoat covered the ensemble. The woman's hair was white and tied in a perfect bun. She was a walking portrait of a librarian stereotype right down to the tiny reading glasses hanging on a petite chain around her wrinkled neck. She wore a blue blouse with a huge collar. The blouse was neatly tucked into her vintage dark green wool pants. The old gentleman fell as he stepped off the curb with his attention skyward instead of where he was stepping. He let go of his wife's hand just in time to keep from pulling her down with him. Ballinger instinctively got out of the car and rushed across the street to help the frail fellow to his feet. The man's chin sported a small gash where he'd hit the pavement. He was a little pale from the sudden fall but seemed to take it all in stride as if it were a common occurrence, which it probably was given his frail stature and old age.

Padilla drove up in the limousine just as Ballinger got the old fellow to his feet. "Wow, must be somebody important coming in for a late lunch," the old timer said as he dabbed at his bleeding chin with a handkerchief. A light rain began to fall as Padilla exited the limo. He left the keys in the ignition and headed straight into the coffee shop. Ballinger wished the old couple well and waited until they were out of sight before retrieving a chauffeur's jacket and hat from his car. He wanted to be sure they didn't see anything to connect him to the limo. If all went according to plan he would soon abandon the luxury ride on some isolated street with the body of Justice Baker in the back seat, then take a cab back to the coffee shop to retrieve his car. He knew Padilla would be expecting the limo back but he really didn't care. He figured Padilla would take a cab home late that night after realizing his limo wasn't coming back.

Ballinger lifted the nine-millimeter Beretta with silencer attached out of the inside pocket of his jacket and put it on the seat beside him. He carefully covered it with the chauffeur's cap. The light rain had turned to a total downpour as he pulled into traffic and headed for Baker's house.

"Are you sure you won't change your mind and come with me this evening?" Baker asked his wife as he took the last sip of an exotic coffee drink he'd made. "I know you just love to hear my speeches."

"Thanks anyway, dear," she replied from the den as she sat sipping her second glass of Domaine Ramonet Montrachet Grand Cru Chardonnay. At just over twelve hundred bucks a bottle it was one of the best in their extensive wine collection. "I've heard enough of your speeches over the years to last ten lifetimes. I'm sure you will be great and probably get a standing ovation."

Baker glanced in the mirror by the front door and adjusted his bow tie just as Ballinger pulled up in the limo. "Don't wait up," he called behind him as he closed the door. He popped open his six-hundred dollar Alexander McQueen umbrella and headed for the limo. Ballinger stepped out and patiently stood in the rain holding the back door open for the good judge. He gave Baker a subtle nod as the adjudicator closed his umbrella and handed it to him. Evelyn Baker sauntered into the luxurious kitchen and poured herself another glass of wine as the limo pulled out of the driveway.

"You're new aren't you? Where's my regular driver? Padilla is his name I think," the judge said as they pulled into traffic.

"Yes sir, I am new to the company. Mr. Padilla was called away on a family emergency. It seems that one of his kids, the younger one I think, fell at school and broke his arm," Ballinger replied as he pushed the button to close the window between himself and his passenger. "Oh, that's too bad," Baker remarked as the window between them slipped close.

Chapter 28

Early Friday evening Addison paid the cab driver and quickly left the cab with her hand shielding her eyebrows from the pouring rain. She was wearing a dark blue Nike gym suit and carrying an oversized gym bag with the unassembled parts of a Barrett M98B sniper rifle, a small tarp and a yoga mat. The bolt action killing machine weighed just over 10 pounds and was a fraction past four feet long when fully assembled. She looked around to make sure the lobby was empty and took the elevator to the fifth floor. A young couple came out of one of the apartments down the hall and walked toward her. She stopped, leaned against the hallway wall, kept her head down and fumbled with her gym bag as if she were looking for something. The couple was busy talking about a party they were on their way to and took no notice of Addison. As soon as the elevator door closed she quickly walked to the roof access ladder at the end of the hall. To her surprise the trap door leading to the roof had no lock of any kind on it. She took a few steps up the ladder, quickly opened the door and tossed the gym bag up on the roof. She finished the short climb up the ladder and crawled onto the wet roof closing the trap door behind her.

The pouring rain had slackened to a light drizzle as she worked her way across the roof looking for the best vantage point from which to take the shot. She found it next to a large HVAC unit. She opened the gym bag and unrolled the yoga mat onto the graveled roof. She assembled the state-of-the-art sniper rifle, laid it on the mat and covered them both with the tarp. She crawled under the tarp, snuggled up to the M98 and looked through the rifle scope carefully studying the kill zone where the Supreme Court Justice would soon be arriving.

Wilder's cab was stuck in traffic a block away from the apartment complex. He got out and quickly jogged into the empty lobby of the Columbia Plaza apartment complex. He hurried across the lobby into the open elevator and punched the button of the fifth floor. Stella the makeup queen was nowhere in sight. As the elevator began to move he reached into the holster located in the small of his back and retrieved his Walther PPK. He jacked a round into the chamber and clicked the safety off before placing the gun back in its holster. The long hallway leading to the roof access ladder was empty. As he reached the top of the ladder he retrieved the Walther and slowly cracked open the access door to the roof. He scanned the roof through the rain looking for signs of Addison. He was beginning to think he'd been mistaken when he caught the smallest glimpse of a rifle barrel just beyond an HVAC unit on the far side of the roof. He quietly climbed through the access door and crept around behind the large unit and came up behind Addison. Addison was so focused on her mission she didn't hear him come up behind her, but somehow she sensed his presence.

"Hello Jack," she said, without moving a muscle while she continued to look through the sniper scope.

"I was hoping you wouldn't figure it out, but I guess I should have known better. You always were pretty smart."

"Don't do it, Addison," he said curtly as he took a shooting stance and pointed his weapon at the back of her head. "You can still get out of this, just stand up and walk away. No one but me has this thing figured out."

"Sorry Jack, they just need to know. The whole country needs to know. Guns are everywhere. We're killing each other, we're killing our children and we're destroying this country that you and I have worked so hard over the years to protect."

"Maybe so," he replied as he moved his finger from the trigger guard to the trigger of his weapon, "but you know if you start to pull that trigger I'll have to kill you and that's not something I want to do." He wasn't very familiar with Baker's politics and even though the guy was kind of a jerk, Jack couldn't let Addison kill him.

Ballinger pulled a handkerchief out of his pocket and began wiping down the dash and steering wheel of the limousine while it idled at a red light. Even though he was wearing leather gloves he wanted to make sure there would be no sign of him being in the vehicle when Baker's body was discovered. He lowered the window between the two compartments. "Nearly there sir," he said as Baker leaned to the right to see around him. "Traffic is a lot heavier than I expected. Just a couple more blocks to go." The judge pulled his speech out of his tuxedo coat pocket, sat back in the seat and began to look it over. He'd given hundreds of these kinds of speeches over his long career. They all had a common theme of how great the country is and how lucky we are to live here instead of some war torn third world hovel. He would also warn about how the country needed to keep an eye on the liberal element in our society who are the greatest internal threat to our democracy and the second amendment.

Addison peered through the scope of the sniper rifle. In the cross hairs she saw her young son Joey smiling and waving at her as he turned and walked into the school building on the last day of his life. She took a deep breath and blinked her eyes. She could see the approaching limo containing her target. She knew her own life was about to end, she just had to somehow stall Wilder long enough for her to pull the trigger. She could see Baker sitting in the back seat reading from some papers he held in front of him. She took two deep breaths as she slowed her heart rate and took aim. In just about three more seconds she would pull the trigger. She figured she had less than a half second after that before her own life would end. In her heart she'd known all along that she couldn't do what she was doing and survive. In the end though she truly felt it was worth it. With both Morgan and Joey gone there was really nothing left to live for. She didn't doubt that Jack would kill her but she figured he would hesitate just enough in his decision to give her time to pull the trigger.

Ballinger pulled to a stop at the next traffic light, picked the Beretta off the seat and turned to face Baker. Baker casually looked up from his notes then gasped as he saw the barrel of the gun pointed directly at his head. Ballinger pulled the trigger as he'd done so many times in the past, instantly killing the Supreme Court justice. But something wasn't right. In the past after the trigger pull there would be a small kickback from the weapon and a muffled sound coming from the barrel of the gun as the bullet headed for its target. This time it was different. Everything was different. The muffled sound wasn't muffled at all. It was very loud and all the oxygen was instantly sucked out of the vehicle before everything went black. Ballinger's mind tried to comprehend what was happening as his spine was severed and the back of his head was torn away by the blast of the bomb that had been planted on the underside of the limousine.

The explosion pushed the 6,000 pound Lincoln Federal Silverstone nearly ten feet straight up, like a rocket on a launch pad. The $75,000 vehicle came back down in two halves, each containing a badly charred, shredded body. The blast rattled buildings and broke windows for a full block. The quiet suburban neighborhood was quickly transformed into a scene of chaos and destruction as survivors in the area ran for cover. Pedestrians closest to the blast were killed instantly or badly maimed from flying glass and other debris. A man in what had been a charcoal gray suit sat on the curb looking down at a severed arm lying in the street in front of him. He turned to look at his left side and realized the arm was his before crumpling forward into the street onto the ghastly limb.

Having been around explosions of all sorts in their careers, both Jack and Addison immediately recognized what had happened. She rolled over on her back and gave Jack a quizzical look. Jack lowered his weapon to his side and shrugged his shoulders as they both ran to the edge of the building and looked down at the chaos.

"Whoa," Jack said. "I didn't see that coming. Was that Baker's limo?"

"Yup," Addison replied. "Another two seconds and I would have taken the shot." Jack knew from the surprised look on her face when the bomb went off that she had no idea it was going to happen. They both stood silently on the edge of the building staring down at the carnage.

After taking in the pandemonium for a minute Jack turned to Addison and said "You know, I'm thinking you had no plan after tonight. You knew I had probably figured it out and you would be dead soon after Baker was. Fact is, someone else beat you to the punch and now you have a second chance. I think the NRA lobbyist case in Eugene is headed for the cold case file. I also think that somewhere in this big wide world there's a tropical island with your name on it. I can just hear those waves calling out to you as they roll up on the sun-filled beach." With that, Wilder turned and silently walked away leaving Addison alone with her thoughts.

Chapter 29

David "Shadow" Wells looked nothing like the guy Jack Wilder had seen in Oregon a few weeks earlier. He was clean shaven, had short hair and was wearing a pair of black rimmed glasses. He could have easily passed for a young college student pursuing studies at nearby George Washington University.

After Wilder had left him in Oregon he became more determined than ever to finish the mission he had started, the mission to end the life of Harold Baker and let people know what a menace Baker had been to society. He'd spent a couple of weeks perfecting the bomb and changing his appearance before making the long trek to Washington D.C. in his old VW bus. After arriving in D.C. he'd managed to land a job on the janitorial crew that cleaned the offices of Fancy Rides Limousine Service. It didn't take long to figure out which limo and driver usually took Baker to his various destinations. After that it was just a matter of picking the right time to attach the bomb to Bakers' limo. At the last minute he made the decision to add another substantial quantity of the C4 explosive to the bomb. He wanted nothing less than the complete destruction of the limo and its occupants. He felt bad for the driver, but collateral damage was inevitable in the war on those who would destroy our environment. The extra explosive had been a careless mistake. Wells should have known better, but his incessant overwhelming desire to destroy Baker had long since usurped any hint of rational thinking on his part. The only thing that mattered was the complete annihilation of Supreme Court Justice Harold Baker and telling the world why he'd done it. His mistake was now costing him his own life as he lay dying on the sidewalk along with several other people who'd been in the wrong place at the wrong time.

He smiled as his breathing became more labored; smiling at the carnage and chaos he'd created. He knew he was dying but it was a small price to pay for what he'd accomplished. Tomorrow the *Washington Post* would no doubt be printing all or at least parts of his manifesto he mailed them a yesterday. Now people would finally sit up and take notice of the things Baker and his cronies were doing to destroy the environment and this great country.

Sarita Padilla was fixing dinner for the kids when a news bulletin interrupted *Wheel of Fortune* which she liked to watch on the small TV on the kitchen counter while she cooked. An explosion had apparently taken the life of Supreme Court Justice Harold Baker and his driver as they were making their way to the Kennedy Center where the Justice was scheduled to give a speech. Sarita's knees collapsed as she screamed and fell to the floor. Both kids came running into the room to see what was happening. "Que Pasa mama, what's wrong?" Carmelita said as she got on her knees and hovered over her distraught mother. Sarita didn't answer, she just sobbed hysterically and pulled both her children close to her. She couldn't believe it. Her Jorge was dead. What had happened? What was she going to do?

Sarita and the children were finally able to get up and go into the living room where they turned on the bigger television and waited for the news. The three of them sat on the overstuffed couch and held each other tightly as the children slowly began to understand what had happened as their mother tried to explain it in between sobs. All three of them were frantic, not knowing what to do or who they could call when the front door of their humble home opened and Jorge walked in. More screams and tears as the family reunited. Jorge sat them down and explained the whole thing from beginning to end as best he could. Carmelita told her father he should call the police and let them know what had happened. "No, mi hija," Jorge said. "They will be able to sort it out themselves."

Wanda Streeter sat at her desk in the Herndon, Virginia Main Post Office on her last day of work. Retirement was only ten minutes away. Wanda is one of those people within the postal system whose job is unique. She gets paid to open other people's mail. Her job title of Mail Recovery Clerk allows her to do so. If a letter is undeliverable, for whatever reason, and has no return address the Mail Recovery Clerk opens the letter and looks at its content to find a clue as to where it came from. There are over six billion such items opened each year by postal employees. That six billion is actually just over 4% of the total

212

items handled annually by the US Postal system. In many cases, when no clue can be found and the contents are deemed to be worth less than twenty-five dollars, the letters are shredded and sent to a recycling center. Those of a higher dollar value are sent to the Mail Recovery Center in Atlanta, Georgia for further investigation or to be auctioned off.

The letter Wanda now held in her hand was addressed to The W.P. 1301 K. Street, Washington D.C. 20170 and had no return address. The zip code 20170 is Herndon, Virginia not Washington D.C. which is why the letter ended up on her desk. "Hmm," she said to herself, "What's W.P? Witness Protection? Water & Power? Some kind of store?" She began looking through the rambling contents of the letter and saw no numbers or names that could have referenced who the sender may have been. What she saw was a lot of stuff about rich people pillaging the land for profit, corrupt politicians and money grubbing people destroying the environment while the EPA sat back and watched. As she perused the letter she missed the part that blamed Supreme Court Justice Harold Baker for a lot of the problems. "Uh, uh, hell no, no way am I gonna spend the last few minutes of my last day looking for something in this mess when there's retirement cake and fruit punch waiting for me in the break room," she thought as she put the sheets back into the envelope and tossed it into the shred bin.

In David Well's exuberant overconfidence he'd casually addressed his manifesto to the W.P. rather than the Washington Post and with just a touch of dyslexia managed to transpose the 20071 zip code into 20170. Right numbers, wrong order. So into the shred-recycle bin in the Herndon, Virginia Post Office it went. That was Wanda Streeter's last official act before heading to the break room for cake and punch after thirty years of loyal service with the United States Postal Service.

Over the next several months the FBI did their usual array of tests and investigations and ultimately traced the explosion to David Wells. Their search into his background turned up a variety of incriminating evidence. This came about as they identified and researched data on all the people killed in the explosion. Their research on Wells ultimately led them to the CREEP organization in Eugene and all the pieces fit. They also, of course, uncovered his association with the limo service that drove Justice Baker to the function that night. The one thing the medical examiner on the case missed was the bullet hole in the center of Baker's forehead. The body was so shredded and badly burned it was an easy miss. The Feds also questioned Wilder about his contact with the CREEPS. They and were satisfied that he was only looking out for the best interest of the Justice and didn't see him as any kind of suspect in the case.

Chapter 30

Balstrop had taken the contract on the Harold Baker hit, compliments of Brian Benavidez, and farmed it out to Ballinger. He and Ballinger had done plenty of business over the years without any complications. Per their agreement, Ballinger would always call immediately after a job was concluded and his pay would be deposited into his Swiss account within 24 hours of the call. On this particular occasion Ballinger did not call. Balstrop made a habit of monitoring various world news reports and knew the job had been completed two days earlier. He'd seen that both the Supreme Court Justice and his limo driver had been killed in a horrendous explosion. He surmised that Ballinger must have been the driver, though he was somewhat surprised. He'd never known Ballinger to use high powered explosives on a job before and he knew Ballinger would never leave any collateral damage. It just wasn't the way Ballinger did things. Balstrop lamented the loss of one of his best operatives for all of two minutes, then gleefully made the decision to keep Ballinger's portion of the proceeds.

George Franklin was out of town looking after one of his real estate developments when the news of Baker's demise reached him. Needless to say, the man was ecstatic about the potential change of the Supreme Court make up. He wasted no time depositing the balance of the money into Balstrop's account.

Later that Spring John "Barney" Fife and Shawn Trotter made a trip back to Eugene, Oregon for a fly fishing trip. It was Trotter's idea. He was determined to learn the sport and had a score to settle with a fir tree on the McKenzie. While they were there they looked up Victoria Miller and compared notes on their respective cases. Both parties agreed that they were looking for the same female killer. The obstacle they faced was not being able to identify who the partial print found at the Eugene murder scene belonged to. As a result, both cases ended up in cold case files.

Jack Wilder sat on his beat up couch in his apartment with his feet up on the coffee table watching *Wheel of Fortune*, pondering his own future. Angus sat quietly on the floor next to the coffee table lapping up the last few drops of beer Jack had poured into his bowl. As Jack sat there staring at Vanna White, she suddenly turned into Addison Cooper. As he watched Addison turn the letters, he wondered if he really could have pulled the trigger and killed her. When they had first met in the Looking Glass unit he was quickly taken with her beauty and under any other circumstances would have passionately pursued her. Now, neither of them held any allegiance to their old employer. He wondered about the possibilities and he wondered if she'd taken his advice.

Addison sat in the shade of a well-worn cabana on one of the beautiful beaches in the French Riviera sipping a French Chardonnay. She'd been there nearly six months and not a day had gone by without her thinking of the loss of her husband and son and how close she came to losing her own life at the hand of a good friend. She wasn't totally sure Jack would have pulled the trigger and, of course, would never know. She wondered if she could have pulled the trigger if their places had been reversed. Somehow she thought not. The more she thought about it, the more she figured there was still much to do. The NRA was still running rampant with vicious attacks on gun control, pouring more money than ever into the pockets of lobbyists and congressmen and women who were too greedy to see what was happening. If she had it to do over again she wouldn't have gone after Baker. She would have spent more time trying to "disarm" the NRA. She took another sip of the excellent wine and wondered if she should try and finish what she had started. If one little weasel with some C4 could take out a Supreme Court Justice, surely someone with her skill and background could take out an entire building or two that housed the NRA. How hard could it be?

A special note to the reader –

The following events gave me the idea for *The Vigilante:*

May 21, 1998 - A shooting at Thurston High School in Springfield, Oregon left two students dead and 25 others wounded by an expelled student. He shot and killed both his parents that same day.

April 20, 1999 - The shooting at Columbine High School in Colorado by two senior students killed a total of 12 students and one teacher.

July 20, 2012 - A gunman sets off tear gas grenades at a Century movie theater in Aurora Colorado, then kills 12 people and injures70 others.

December 14, 2012 - A twenty year old fatally shoots 20 children and 6 adult staff members at Sandy Hook Elementary School, in Newtown Connecticut.

December 11, 2012 - A twenty-two year old opens fire in a shopping mall outside of Portland Oregon, killing two people and seriously wounding a third.

May 23, 2014 - A young shooter in Isla Vista, California kills 7 and wounds 13 before taking his own life, leaving three semi-automatic handguns and more than 400 rounds of ammunition at his side.

September 2013 - Two Colorado Democrats who provided crucial support for a package of state gun law controls are voted out of office in special election.

The NRA isn't just blocking new gun law, it's going after laws elected representatives have already passed. The shooting in Isla Vista came as the NRA continues its assault on attempts to tighten gun laws, and on laws currently in place.

Lastly, the Newtown tragedy took the lives of so many innocent young children and several adults. You see that event thinly disguised in this book. None of us can ever understand the horror and emotional trauma those people are going through.

This is a small sample of the rampant carnage that plagues our country today. Think about it........ something needs to be done.

Acknowledgements

Thanks very much to Shawn Trotter for once again letting me use your name and expertise. I hope you enjoyed your character. Thanks Phil Johnson, my best fly fishing buddy, for the use of your name as well, I hope you enjoyed your character. A huge thanks to Aven Wright-McIntosh for her super editing skills of each draft and to Carla Grenier for her proof reading skills. Lastly thanks to my wonderful wife Pat for her suggestions, criticisms, encouragement, and editing skills.

Turn the page for a preview of W.R. Hill's first thriller *The Oil Conspiracy* followed by an excerpt from the spellbinding short story *Déjà vu in Blue.*

The Oil Conspiracy

Chapter 1

Ballinger left his hotel at five that morning dressed in workout sweats, carrying a gym bag stuffed with the disassembled Barret M82A1 sniper rifle, a Glock 17 and a change of clothes. As a Marine sniper in Iraq, he killed for love of country. Now he kills for love of money.

The weather was typical for a February in Vienna, very cold in the mornings warming to the mid-forties by afternoon. The sky was overcast and a light fog was creeping in from the Danube. A slight mist hung in the air as he walked down damp empty streets. The street lights shined a pale yellow in the fog. Ballinger pulled the hood up on his sweatshirt to ward off the morning chill. He walked the six blocks to the Zurich building looking like any other gym rat headed to his early morning workout. He had an angular face, stood a little over six feet tall and weighed in at 220. With scant body fat and muscles reinforced by steroids, he could have passed as a wide receiver with the Dallas Cowboys. He looked a lot like that guy Howie what's-his-name, the football sportscaster, only without the fifties flat top haircut.

He stopped next to the building, gave the periphery a quick glance and ducked into the dark alley. The space between the man-made monoliths was filled with molding trash bags, cigarette butts, fast food wrappers and empty cardboard boxes, all crammed against a couple of rusting dumpsters. He pulled on a pair of latex gloves and opened the lid on the dumpster nearest the Zurich building. then, he picked the lock on the delivery door and went inside. In the dim light of the shipping area he disabled the proximity alarm well within the thirty seconds it took to register an intrusion. He stepped into the utility elevator, punched the button for the executive floor and hummed *Margaritaville* to himself on the ride up. When the doors opened, he crossed to enter the stairwell and noted the fire alarm box on the wall. *Perfect* he thought to himself. He took the stairs two at a time up one flight. He came to a long hallway with a ladder to the roof attached to the wall at the end. He climbed the ladder, opened the hatch and stepped into the cool crisp air on the roof.

Ballinger stood motionless in the darkness surrounded by the early morning silence. He surveyed the roof. Six HVAC units stood like giant sentries at their posts silently keeping watch over the city. They were painted a dark gray with spots of rust at the corners brought on by harsh wet winters and dry summers. As his eyes adjusted to the dim light, he settled in behind the unit giving the clearest view of the OPEC building's southwest door some 750 yards away. He sat still in the crisp morning darkness visualizing what was to come, acquiring the target, taking the shot, the ensuing chaos and making his exit.

Twelve stories below as the sun crept over the horizon pushing its way through the clouds and morning mist, Vienna came to life. Early morning delivery trucks dropped off goods to shops and cafes. The smell of fresh breads and other pastries being baked wafted through the streets. Bundles of newspapers hit street corners, to be retrieved by sleep weary vendors and sold in small downtown shops. In a few more hours the city would be a bustling hub of activity.

Ballinger began the rifle assembly. The Barret M82A1weighs just under thirty pounds and is four feet long fully assembled. It shoots a .50 caliber bullet that leaves the barrel traveling 2,799 feet per second. The weapon is accurate up to a distance of just over 1,900 yards. At a cost of $8,900 each, the U.S. Marine Corps bought 125 of them for use in Desert Shield and Desert Storm in Kuwait and Iraq. Your tax dollars at work.

Ballinger grew up the youngest of four brothers, each of whom had a different father. His mother, Louise was an attractive and extremely intelligent woman. She would generally bring home men of lesser intelligence who were easily manipulated. A couple of them actually married her. She used them up, got what she wanted, usually in the form of cash or real estate and sent them packing. There were a few live-in lovers as well who quickly met the same fate.

Louise moved often, always taking the kids with her which meant they'd be out of school for months at a time. Most of the kids' fathers never knew where they were and probably didn't care. Louise never had any real interest in being a parent. She was totally focused on herself. All the boys were pretty much left to raise themselves. As the youngest, Ballinger was often picked on by his older half brothers and by the older kids at the six different schools he went to in his six years of elementary school. When he got to high school he enjoyed a growth spurt that made him one of the biggest kids in the school. He spent a great deal of time in detention, always in trouble, mostly for fighting. He particularly enjoyed going after cheerleader boyfriends. These were the kind of guys who got the attention he craved growing up. He would flirt with the girls, their boyfriends would get angry and a fight would ensue. Ballinger always won, usually with only one punch, occasionally a second one was required, but that was rare.

Toward the end of his senior year a guidance counselor suggested the military might bring him the discipline and focus lacked. He joined the Marines the day after graduation and never looked back.

Ballinger found that the Marines did, indeed, provide him with the discipline and focus he needed. He also developed a sense of self worth and a love of his country, a love ultimately ruined by kiss-ass officers at the highest levels who never saw a day of combat. They made poor decisions, on a daily basis, costing hundreds of lives, including those of some of his closest friends. His fellow Marines became the family he always wanted but never had. The Marine discipline and focus also turned him into a finely tuned, highly efficient killing machine. It was the perfect release for years of pent up anger and rage over the continual neglect in his life.

He finished the sniper rifle assembly, attached the bi-pod to the barrel just above the stock and gently laid the weapon down like a mother returning a new born to its crib. It would take less than three quarters of a second for the bullet to travel from the top of the Zurich building to the southwest door of the OPEC building.

Chapter 2

Forty-five year old Trinidad Palacios, "Trini" to his friends, had sunken cheekbones, a pointed nose, and stood a shade over six feet. His gaunt frame and lanky stature made his facial features even more prominent. He had a thinning and rapidly receding hairline and wore thick wire-rimmed glasses. All in all, he looked like a living caricature of the Ichabod Crane character in Washington Irving's short story about the headless horseman.

A light rain was falling outside as Trini sat at his desk in the study of the family's opulently furnished OPEC apartment. His employers spared no expense when it came to the comforts of home. The spacious apartment had three bedrooms, a gourmet kitchen and expensive antique European furniture dotted every room. The luxurious living quarters were kept clean by a maid who came in twice a week.

The complex included an onsite gym, frequented by his wife to maintain her absolutely perfect figure. Trini often wondered how a man of his looks and body ended up with such a beauty. When he would ask his wife about it she would laugh it off and reply that his inner beauty, caring and sensitivity were all she could ever want in a member of the opposite sex.

The only room not neat and tidy in the entire apartment was Trini's study. It looked like a library that had been hit by a tornado. There were layers of scientific papers on every surface available. The shelves held books stacked every which way imaginable. Mountains of books and papers sat on the floor, abandoned long ago for more up to date publications. A few half empty coffee cups and a dozen or so partially eaten pastries added a moldy touch of color to the chaotic ambience. To anyone else the room looked like a disaster area waiting for the Red Cross to arrive. To Trini it was carefully organized chaos.

He had been up since four a.m. reading all the documents he carried home from his office the night before. Even though he had read them all hundreds of times, he still found it hard to believe. Yet, the truth lay there on his desk, staring up at him like a coiled snake readying to strike. A conspiracy of this magnitude was unfathomable. How could it have happened? Who could have orchestrated it?

There were copies of memos, emails and cables sent to various people from all around the world. Many were from OPEC countries. Individually they didn't point to much at all. But looked at as a whole, it was clear a conspiracy had been carefully and meticulously designed and put into place. Trini spent nearly six months calling in favors, bribing clerks and snooping through computers and trash bins long after ordinary business hours ended. He had carefully assembled all the pieces of the puzzle. The world oil shortage crisis that was growing larger each day was all a sham.

As an analyst for OPEC, one of his main functions was to monitor and report on world oil production. For nearly eight months, several OPEC countries had been cutting oil production and it had peaked Trini's curiosity. It just didn't make sense. Based on previous reports, Trini was confident there were ample amounts of oil, above and below ground, in all the OPEC countries. Yet, the cut back had happened. Saudi Arabia was the first, followed by Iran, Iraq, Venezuela and Kuwait. The results worldwide were disastrous. Europeans already used to paying high prices for their petrol were outraged and U.S. consumers were starting to see prices climb well above five dollars a gallon. Crude oil had reached an all time high of one hundred-seventy dollars a barrel. Many cities in Europe and the U.S. were implementing gas rationing. Banks the world over were repossessing gas guzzling vehicles at an alarming rate. Consumers could no longer afford large car and truck payments equivalent to the cost of a tank of gas.

At first, the larger oil producing countries cut production by five percent. The last set of data showed that some of them had cut production by nearly 20 percent over the previous eight months, and all of them were claiming that several of their wells had run dry.

It appeared that the conspiracy had been put together by some of the people Trini worked with at OPEC. He realized he had to put a stop to the madness. His plan was to make the announcement at the press conference scheduled that afternoon. These press conferences were routine when OPEC meetings were in session. And given the alleged crisis, the world press was eager for any morsel OPEC might offer. While Trini had done his best to cover his tracks and keep his findings a secret, he knew he couldn't be absolutely sure no one else knew about his discovery.

Trini also knew that if he told the higher ups at OPEC he would find himself out on the street, out of a job, and labeled a crackpot in short order. After several long and sleepless nights he felt the best thing, the only thing he could do, was to make the announcement and let the chips fall where they may. If he was going to be out of a job anyway, he was going to go out with a clear conscience.

He picked up the documents, stuffed them into an envelope and addressed it to his old friend and colleague, Garrison Shepherd, in Houston, Texas. Trini and Garrison had worked together at Global Oil in Houston before Trini had landed his dream job at

OPEC. They had similar scientific backgrounds and ideas about the future of oil in the world. Trini and Garrison had quickly become good friends and often helped each other on various complex projects they were assigned at Global. Trini figured the information he was sending to Garrison would serve as an insurance policy in the event that something happened. He knew Garrison would do the right thing with the information if it ever came to that. Trini swallowed the last drop of cold coffee from one of the many cups on his desk and hastily scribbled a note to his wife asking her to drop the package off at the Post Office on her way to the market later that day. He made a quick call to Garrison, got his voice mail, and left a message telling him to expect an important package, one they would talk about later in greater detail.

Trini left his apartment at six-forty five that morning, an hour earlier than usual, and headed to his office. Before leaving, he kissed his wife and two sleepy kids goodbye. He assured the entire family that wild horses couldn't keep him from attending his son's soccer match that afternoon and his daughter's ballet recital that evening. The OPEC limo was waiting for him in the circular drive of the residence. The driver, a stocky guy with a sullen scarred face, held the door open as Trini climbed in. The early morning fog was beginning to clear and a glimmer of sun was slowly pushing its way through the heavy cloud cover. It was a day Trini hoped would become brighter still after he made his announcement. The driver climbed in, looked in the rear view mirror and pulled into the light morning traffic. They arrived at OPEC headquarters just past seven.

Trini poured himself a fresh cup of coffee and closed the door to his cluttered office, a close replica of his chaotic home office, right down to the stale pastries. He spent the next two hours rehearsing what he was going to say at the press briefing. He had nothing in writing, everything had been sent to Garrison. He didn't want anyone discovering what he was going to say. He viewed his discovery as a matter of providing economic stability to a world that was rapidly falling apart. Someone had to do something, and he was that someone.

Trini rose from his chair, stood next to his desk, took a deep breath and headed for the door. He walked quickly through the building, with an intense focus on the task at hand. He was a man on a mission, oblivious to the people and things around him. It was exactly ten-fifteen that morning when he walked through the door at the southwest corner of the OPEC building. The limo driver was waiting patiently, holding the door of the vehicle open for his passenger. The destination was the Vienna Hilton where the world press would be given details about the bogus oil shortage. Trini had a clear head and a precise vision of what he was going to say. He was confident he had come to the right decision.

The Oil Conspiracy **Now Available on Amazon.com**

For more information on author W.R. Hill visit:

www.wrhill.com

Déjà vu in Blue

One

A light rain was beginning to fall at 11:00 p.m. on September the 20th 1985, as officer Dan Armstrong walked out of the his favorite coffee shop on West Seventh delicately balancing a cup of hot coffee in one hand and his notebook and keys in the other. He'd spent most of the last two hours craving a great cup of coffee to give him that extra boost of energy he needed as he eased into the late shift. He slid behind the wheel of his cruiser car, dropped his notebook on the passenger seat, keyed the mic and said "Victor two-nine code 12" indicating he was back in service and ready for assignment. The dispatcher's voice immediately came back, "Victor two-nine, two-eleven in progress, 7-Eleven convenience store 951 West Sixth. " Two-eleven was the code for robbery in progress.

"Victor two-nine en route," Armstrong responded. He rolled his window down with his left hand, tossed the full cup of coffee out the window and hit the switch for the light bar. He slammed the shiny new Ford Crown Vic into reverse, lurched out of the parking lot, headed east on seventh, turned left

231

on Monroe then left on sixth. He flipped off the light bar as he made the last turn, drove two more blocks and turned into the driveway of the old motel next to the convenience store. The entire trip took about thirty seconds.

Armstrong turned off the headlights of his cruiser as he pulled into the empty motel parking lot stopping at a space farthest away from the convenience store. Ten seconds later 15- year veteran Landry Dixon pulled his cruiser up next to Armstrong's. Dixon was six-three and weighed a solid two forty-five. In his fifteen years on the force Dixon had seen more than his share of action and had the physical and mental scars to prove it. You name it, he'd lived it; domestics, bar fights, high speed chases, physical take downs, assaults, robberies and the list went on. He also held the department record for marksmanship.

"Hey Danny boy, what's shakin'?" Dixon asked as he got out and opened the trunk of his cruiser and retrieved his KG-99 assault rifle.

"You know, same old stuff," Armstrong replied as he pulled his service revolver from its holster.

"You go east and I'll go west," Dixon said as the two of them stood there double checking their weapons and ammunition.

Armstrong nodded and slowly made his way along the six foot high block wall that separated the motel parking lot from the convenience store lot. Dixon walked down the alley behind the little market and made his way along the west side to the front corner of the building. Armstrong rounded the end of the wall and slowly made his way up to the building, hugging the wall as he crept along. He glanced up at the sky. The rain had increased and a slight wind carried a chill along with the dampness. He turned his jacket collar up with his free hand as he slowly made his way toward the front of the building.

He could see the terrified clerk in the store standing behind the counter as he rounded the corner of the building. She had her hands in the air and her upper body was bent backwards trying to put as much distance as she could between her and the gun pointed at her chest. She looked to be college age with light blonde hair pulled back in a pony tail. Her hands were shaking as she stared at the guy pointing the gun at her. The thug was reaching across the counter with his left hand pulling money out of the open cash drawer and shoving it into his jacket pocket. The gun in his right hand waved back and forth across her body as he struggled to get the cash. Armstrong looked around and saw only one car in the parking lot, a beat up Toyota with the passenger side window rolled down. It appeared to be empty. He didn't see the lone occupant lying down in the front seat.

A few seconds later the robber burst out of the store's front door. "Police! Drop your weapon!" Armstrong shouted from the corner of the building as the robber looked in his direction. From the opposite corner of the building Dixon saw a lone gunman rise up from the seat of the Toyota and fire at Armstrong through the open window hitting him squarely in his side just beneath his armpit. Dixon pivoted, aimed his KG-99 at the shooter and put three quick shots through the windshield into his chest, then turned back and put two more into the guy standing in the front door of the store who now had his weapon raised and poised to fire. "Officer down! Officer down!" Dixon shouted into his shoulder mic as he ran towards the Toyota with his KG-99 trained on the vehicle. He quickly confirmed the threat had been eliminated then ran to the store front and kicked the robber's weapon out of reach as the guy lay on the sidewalk, his dead eyes staring straight up at the falling rain. Then he ran to Armstrong's prone body. "Hang on, Danny," he said as he turned him over. As soon as he turned him he could tell he was gone. He had been killed instantly with a lucky shot to his side. A few inches either way and his vest would have taken the impact. Dixon had killed both bad guys and would later receive a commendation for his heroic actions. Justice had been served but a fine officer had been lost in the process.

Officer Dan Armstrong, badge number 1094, had been a policeman exactly five years that night. Just a few hours earlier he had been home with his family celebrating his son Alex's fifth birthday. Dan Armstrong, like most men in his family line, had always wanted to be a policeman. He had made the grade and given his all.

It was a little after two in the morning when five-year-old Alex Armstrong heard the doorbell ring. He had been dreaming about all the cool things he had gotten for his birthday. There were two sets of Legos and several other things, but the best gift of all was a plastic police officer badge along with a set of toy handcuffs from his dad. He crawled out from under his Captain America blanket and stood at the top of the stairs straining to hear what was being said. He couldn't make out what the voices were saying as he blinked the sleep from his eyes and tried to listen. The one thing he clearly heard was his mother scream as she started sobbing and dropped to her knees. The Police Chief and an assistant stepped into the room and helped his mother to her feet and over to the couch. She was sobbing hysterically. Alex quickly made his way downstairs to his mother's side. She saw him and pulled him tightly to her chest, wet from the flood of tears. "Oh Alex, Alex, Alex," was all she could manage to say as she sobbed and rocked back and forth with her arms tightly wrapped around her son. Alex clung to his grieving mother as his five-year-old mind tried to make sense of what was happening.

Two

The day was ice cold and snow was in the forecast as Alex stood silently staring at his mother's coffin. Five years earlier he'd been at his dad's funeral and now here he was staring at his mother's coffin as she was about to be laid to rest next to her beloved husband. He held his Aunt's hand and looked up at her as she dabbed tears from her eyes. She pulled him closer to ward off the chill. Alex looked around the cemetery as he stood there shivering in the cold. There were headstones as far as he could see in every direction. He looked at the long row of cars tucked in behind the hearse that had carried his mother's casket to this cold, dreary place. There were several police cars in the line driven by cops who came to pay their respects. They were friends of Alex's dad who had kept in touch over the years since his dad's death. They had often dropped by to check on him and his mom. The first one to offer condolences was Landry Dixon, the officer who had been with Alex's dad the night he was killed. Each one came up to Alex, told him how sorry they were and gave him a hug.

His mother had died five days earlier, oddly enough, on his tenth birthday. He had been asleep in his room when his Aunt woke him to say his mom was gone, her suffering had come to an end. The cancer that had been diagnosed in February of that year had quickly spread to several vital organs. Soon after she realized nothing could be done to save her, she and Alex moved in with her sister Maxine.

As Alex stood there in the cold the words the preacher had spoken a little earlier in the church came floating back to him. "Nelda Jo Armstrong was born on the ninth of September, 1957. She died on September 20th, 1995. She is survived by her son Alex Armstrong and her sister Maxine Grissom. Her husband, Dan preceded her in death." Alex shifted his attention back to the preacher who was now standing at the head of the casket reading a passage from the Bible.

Alex's mother had lived long enough to make arrangements for him to live with his Aunt Maxine after she was gone. His mother and he had many long conversations about what his future might hold for him after she was gone. She had hopes that he would become a doctor or a lawyer. Alex said he would think about it, all the while knowing that all he wanted was to be a policeman like his father. Deep down, despite her hopes, his mother knew he would turn out to be a cop. Whatever happened and whatever he would become, she took comfort knowing her sister Maxine would do a great job of raising her son after she was gone.

After the funeral they returned to his Aunt's house where Alex stood and watched as casseroles, sandwiches and desserts came parading through the front door. The only place he'd ever seen so much food was in one of those all-you-can-eat cafeteria places. He walked by the dining room table scanning all the food. He figured he and his Aunt had enough food to last a lifetime.

When the last well wisher left, his Aunt went into her room, kicked off her shoes and collapsed on the bed. Alex could hear her sobbing as he passed by her closed door. He started to go in, but hesitated and turned away. Instead, he went to his own room, opened the bottom drawer of his dresser and took out the plastic handcuffs and police badge. He carried them over to his bed and turned them over and over in his small hands as he lay staring at the ceiling. Why, he thought, why has God taken everyone away from me? He became angry at the thought of it all. He threw the badge and handcuffs across the room, rolled over and sobbed loudly into his pillow. The pillow was soaked with tears when he finally fell asleep.

Days turned into weeks and months as Alex and his Aunt grieved the loss of mother and sister. Grief, like guilt diminishes over time but never completely goes away. They both eventually settled into their lives and routines. Alex was now more determined than ever to become a policeman. There were bad guys out there who needed to be in jail and he was going to put them there. He threw himself into everything he did with a vengeance. He made excellent grades all through school and proved himself to be a superb athlete in every sport. All the girls in school swooned over him but he showed little interest. He was focused and driven as he marched toward his goal of becoming a police officer. His wonderful aunt supported him with all her heart in his every endeavor.

After high school Alex attended the local community college where he earned an Associate Degree in Criminal Justice. As soon as he was old enough he submitted the lengthy application to the Eugene Police Department. He scored the highest possible points every step of the way through the hiring process and soon found himself at the Police Academy. His dream was becoming a reality.

Three

Eugene police officer Alex Armstrong smiled as he slid behind the door of his 2005-365 horsepower Ford Intercept to start his shift. He put the Ford in gear, took a deep breath and said to himself, *I made it, I am a policeman.* This was it, September 20th 2005. It's what he'd been working towards his entire life. Alex thought back to that terrible night when his dad had been killed. He looked up and said "I made it Dad; I hope you're proud of me." Life was good; he had gotten his degree, met and married a wonderful woman and graduated from the Police Academy at the top of his class. He had a beautiful son who had been born the day he graduated and now for the first time, his training officer had cut him loose to drive on his own.

Alex keyed the mic. "Adam two-one in service." The department had long ago abandoned the old code system in favor of "plain talk" doing away with the sometimes confusing codes.

"Adam two-one in service," came the response from the dispatcher.

Alex put the cruiser in gear and headed for the streets.

He waved at some kids skateboarding on the sidewalk as he drove down a quiet street in one of the neighborhoods he patrolled. Tree leaves were beginning to change color and the temperature hovered in the high sixties. Not much going on, a slow day in the hood. He had stopped to watch some kids playing baseball in an empty field when his radio crackled.

"Adam two-one, see the woman about an animal in distress, 984 Sheraton." Not wanting to be attacked by some wild animal he radioed back, "Do we know what kind of animal and what kind of distress?"

"Adam two-one, woman states her cat is underneath the house and won't come out. Animal control officer unavailable at this time."

"Adam two-one en route."

Really? Really? Alex thought to himself. *I'm a police officer with a big gun sworn to protect and serve and my first call is to rescue a cat?* He drove to the closest grocery store, purchased a can of tuna and headed to the woman's house. A short, elderly, significantly overweight woman wearing black pants a size too small with a bright neon green top was frantically pacing back and forth as he pulled up to the residence. She looked like a giant colorful beach ball with a head.

"Oh, thank goodness you're here," the woman said. "I'm Mabel, Mabel Grisham. Gertrude, well I call her Gertie, but her actual name is Gertrude, is under the house and refuses to come out. She keeps meowing like there is something wrong. I'm afraid some kind of animal is under there holding her hostage or something. Did you bring your gun?"

"Sounds pretty serious," Alex said as he got out of the cruiser. "Can you show me where Gertie went under the house?"

The portly woman quickly waddled across the yard and pointed to a small opening next to the front porch. "That's it, that's the spot," she said as she pointed to the small opening. Alex opened the can of tuna, set it in front of the opening and stepped back.

Two minutes later the head of the cat appeared at the entrance. Gertrude was orange and white with white sox on all four feet. Her two front paws each had seven toes. "Oh Gertie, you naughty cat," the woman said as she scooped the feline into her arms.

"Oh Officer Armstrong," the woman said as she looked at Alex's badge and squinted, I can't thank you enough."

"Glad to be of service," Alex said as he climbed back into his cruiser and radioed himself back into action.

As he drove off he realized the cat lady somehow reminded him of his mother who had passed away a few years after his dad was killed. His mother wasn't that overweight by a long shot, but there was still something there that reminded him of her. He couldn't quite put his finger on it, but it seemed to be something about the way the woman smiled as she thanked him. It was the kind of smile Alex had seen many times on his mother's face before his dad died, a smile that died with him.

A few weeks later Alex found himself sitting on the couch in Auntie Max's spacious living room bouncing William, his eight month old son on his knee. His wife Audrie and his aunt fluttered about in the kitchen preparing dinner. Over the years Maxine had become a wonderful matronly woman whose glasses were always worn on the tip of her nose. When she talked she would tilt her chin down and look at you over the top of those old wire-rim spectacles. She wore her gray hair in a perpetual bun wound tightly on the back of her head. She had never married. "The right guy just never came along, at least not yet," she'd say with a twinkle in her eye whenever she was asked about her marital status. Maxine had always supported Alex in his laser focused drive to become a policeman. She did this despite her misgivings about the dangers Alex would face as a police officer, knowing that both his father and grandfather had been policemen killed in the line of duty. Nevertheless, Auntie Max provided him with all the love and support any mother could ever have given.

Pleasant smells of pot roast and potatoes wafted through the living room as Alex and the baby played while a very old Grandfather clock next to an even older upright piano kept watch from the corner of the room. The top of the piano was covered with framed memories of family gatherings from years gone by. There were pictures of Alex coming home from the hospital when he was a few days old, pictures of Alex's dad graduating from the Police Academy, pictures of Alex's parents on their wedding day and of course, pictures of Alex at his Police Academy graduation.

Audrie was 25 years old, a natural blonde with dimples the size of Cleveland and blue eyes that could charm even the most hardcore curmudgeon. She was a shade over five-two and wore a size 5 in everything except shoes. She and Alex had one of those whirlwind courtships. They met while Alex was working at the local Home Depot in the paint department while he waded through the lengthy process of physical and mental testing, interviews, written tests, and a host of odd psychological evaluations to see if he fit the criteria to become a police officer. Despite the grueling process Alex was never in doubt about the outcome. After all, he had police genes passed down from his father and grandfather. William had been born nine months to the day after the last night of their short honeymoon.

"Soup's on!" Auntie Max hollered from the dining room as she and Audrie set the last of the scrumptious meal on the table. They all ate until they were about to explode, then politely listened as Maxine told stories about days gone by and the adventures of Alex's father and grandfather.

"I'll never forget," Auntie said as she squelched a small burp, "about your dad's first night on his own as a police officer. He was so excited and handsome in his new blue uniform. I think the blue uniforms they wear today are better looking though. I never liked that stripe thing that went down the outside of the pant legs. Anyway, he was ready for action." She paused as she took a sip of the freshly brewed coffee that had accompanied her famous pecan pie. "He was ready for anything and his very first call was to go and see some goofy woman whose cat had gone underneath her house and refused to come out. He said the short woman was about as wide as she was tall and wore pants a size or two smaller than they should have been. Of course the animal control guy was nowhere to be found so your Dad's first big assignment was to get a cat out from under a house." She paused to take a breath and another sip of coffee. "Well" she said, "your Dad, being the smart guy he was, figured what cat can resist a can of tuna right? So he stops by the store, picks up a can of tuna and sets it outside the opening that goes under the house.

Don't ya know it wasn't two minutes until that stupid cat came a runnin. Yep, your dad was a hero on his first day by himself. Not a get-a-medal hero, just a hero to the goofy woman with the silly cat. As I recall, the cat even had a weird name, Gertrude or something like that I think it was."

Déjà vu in Blue **Now Available on Amazon.com**

For more information on author W.R. Hill visit:

www.wrhill.com

70593707R00148

Made in the USA
Columbia, SC
09 May 2017